Puffin Books

# The Flying Emu

## and other Australian stories

What happened to Marni, the girl who couldn't stop shouting?

How did Marlu the kangaroo and Willie the wagtail get to be such great friends?

What about the boy who nearly wished his life away?

And can you *really* have a gourmet giant?

*The Flying Emu and other Australian stories* will tell you the answer to these – and many other strange questions. Enter a world of magic and imagination, of unexpected happenings and some very eccentric characters.

Other books by Sally Morgan

*My Place*
*Wanamurraganya*
*Little Piggies*
*Hurry Up, Oscar*
*Pet Problem*
*Dan's Grandpa*
*The Art of Sally Morgan*

# The Flying Emu

## and other Australian stories

## SALLY MORGAN

Puffin Books

Puffin Books
Penguin Books Australia Ltd
487 Maroondah Highway, PO Box 257
Ringwood, Victoria 3134, Australia
Penguin Books Ltd
Harmondsworth, Middlesex, England
Penguin Putnam Inc.
375 Hudson Street, New York, New York 10014, USA
Penguin Books Canada Limited
10 Alcorn Avenue, Toronto, Ontario, Canada, M4V 3B2
Penguin Books (N.Z.) Ltd
Cnr Rosedale and Airborne Roads, Albany, Auckland, New Zealand
Penguin Books (South Africa) (Pty) Ltd
5 Watkins Street, Denver Ext 4, 2094, South Africa
Penguin Books India (P) Ltd
11, Community Centre, Panchsheel Park, New Delhi 110 017, India

First published by Viking, 1992
This edition first published, 1997
5 7 9 10 8 6 4

Copyright © Sally Morgan, 1992

Typeset in 12/15 Veljovic by Bookset Type & Image, Victoria
Made and printed in Australia by Australian Print Group,
Maryborough, Victoria

National Library of Australia
Cataloguing-in-Publication data:

Morgan, Sally, 1951– .
The flying emu and other Australian stories.

(New ed.).
ISBN 0 14 038191 0.

I. Title

A823.3

www.puffin.com.au

# Contents

# Preface

My people, the indigenous people of Australia, have a tradition of story-telling that extends over thousands and thousands of years. I was brought up in a family where story-telling was an important part of our life. The stories you will read in this book are not traditional ones, but some of them were drawn from my own childhood, while others were suggested by the interests of my children and nieces and nephews.

One of my fondest memories as a child is of lying outside on the grass, with an old rug pulled over me, listening to my mother tell us stories. When she ran out of ideas she'd point up to the stars and we'd talk about them. Then we'd have a sing-song, which generally went on until we lost our voices or fell asleep. One of our favourite ways of telling stories was for someone to begin and then another to continue the story. My brothers always made their part of the story as rude as Mum would allow.

My grandmother introduced me to the idea of bush creatures having their own stories to tell. I remember once crawling up as close as I dared to a goanna and thinking seriously about what it might say if it could speak. At other times I would hunt for fairies and elves under the big nasturtium leaves, convinced that these beings were bound to be doing something that would interest me.

Whenever I was bored or unhappy I would drift off into another world that was inhabited by all sorts of intriguing creatures. There I would have great adventures. And of course I was always the heroine!

These stories are dedicated to all the naughty children in the world, but most especially to the Aboriginal children of Australia, who are some of the greatest story-tellers of all.

# The flying emu

**E**mu was once the most colourful bird in Australia. His head feathers were brilliant blue, his huge wings were shades of pink and purple, his body was like spun gold, and his big feet were bright red with lime-green claws. While some of the other birds thought Emu was a bit much, Emu loved himself.

'I'm so handsome!' he sighed as he gazed at his reflection in the still waters of the billabong. He leant down closer to the surface and burst into song:

I love my rainbow feathers,
I love my great, big wings,
I love the way my eyes shine,
I'm a wonderful handsome thing!

Then he pursed his beak and made a long, drawn-out kissing sound.

Frog surfaced suddenly in the middle of Emu's reflection and croaked, 'Emu old buddy, how are you today?' Frog was a great admirer of Emu and had been trying to make friends with him for a long time.

'Buzz off, Froggy', Emu hissed. 'You're spoiling my view!'

Frog felt quite hurt at that. 'Don't you want any friends?' he asked.

Emu laughed nastily. 'Why would I want friends when I have myself?' he sneered. This made Frog feel very sad so he dived back under the water.

Now Kookaburra, a bird known for his mocking laugh, was watching from a nearby tree. He was very jealous of Emu and had been planning a way to get rid of him for a long time.

'Now is the perfect moment to put my little plan into action', he muttered to himself. He called out loudly, 'You're quite right, Emu – Frog is as dull as mud. Whereas your brilliance can only be compared to the shining noonday sun!'

Emu kept staring at his own reflection, but

just for a moment he smiled encouragingly at
Kookaburra. Emu loved compliments.

'Your wings are like twin rainbows', continued
Kookaburra. 'Your head is a sparkling sapphire
and your feet are radiant rubies.'

Emu nodded proudly. It was all true.

'I'm so dull', Kookaburra sighed sadly. 'When I
sing everyone thinks I'm laughing at them.'

Emu nodded in agreement. He didn't think
much of Kookaburra either. He smiled contentedly at his own reflection again and once more
burst into song:

> What a wonderful bird I am!
> What a wonderful bird I am!
> Forget the rest 'cause I'm the best!
> Yes, I'm the handsomest.

Kookaburra felt sickened by Emu's vanity, but
he managed to say smoothly, 'What a tune, what a
voice'.

Emu chuckled smugly. Really, there was no
end to his talents.

'I'll never be as glorious as you', sighed Kookaburra sadly. 'Thank heaven I can fly fast and high,
otherwise I'd have nothing at all to boast about.'

Emu tilted his head and asked curiously, 'Are
you saying I can't fly fast and high?'

'Of course not!' replied Kookaburra. 'It's just

that I'm so small compared with you. I don't have a giant body or giant feet to weigh me down.'

Emu looked at his feet. They were big. But then, he reasoned, a magnificent body needed magnificent feet and legs to carry it.

While Emu continued to gaze adoringly at his feet, Kookaburra squashed a laugh. His plan was working well and he didn't want to spoil it by laughing out of turn.

'Feet aren't really important', he said as he interrupted Emu's thoughts. 'Wings are the main thing.'

Emu nodded and puffed out his chest. Then, in a moment of great pride, he spread out his glorious wings to their full span.

'Oh marvellous, marvellous!' admired Kookaburra. 'What an honour to see such a sight.' He spread out his own small brown and white wings, but Emu laughed nastily and said, 'I wouldn't bother if I were you'.

Kookaburra quickly pulled his wings in and said, 'I know my wings aren't twin rainbows, but I *can* fly fast and high. I could even fly to the sun if I wanted to'.

'Fly to the sun', Emu scoffed. 'You're not only dull but stupid too!'

'You can insult me as much as you like', taunted Kookaburra, 'but that won't change the fact that while my wings are small and light, yours are big and heavy. It's only logical that I must be able to fly faster and higher than you'.

Emu was outraged. What a nasty, horrible little bird Kookaburra was.

'You haven't got a brain in your head!' hissed Emu angrily.

'That may be so', said Kookaburra, 'but that still doesn't mean you can fly to the sun. You're just too big and fat!'

'I am not!' screeched Emu. 'I can beat you at anything, any day, any time. I challenge you to a flying contest tomorrow at dawn.'

Kookaburra shook his head. 'No good', he said. 'I will only accept your challenge if we fly at noon. That way everyone can see me win. And I want to go first!'

'Oh no you're not!' objected Emu. 'It's my challenge so I'll go first. Noon it is!'

Kookaburra was so excited that Emu had fallen so easily into his trap that he couldn't help emitting a small, mocking laugh, 'Haa, haa . . .'

'What was that?' asked Emu suspiciously.

'Aah, aah . . . nothing. I was just clearing my throat.'

Emu sent him a withering glance and then returned to looking at himself in the billabong.

Kookaburra, feeling very pleased with himself, flew off to find a resting place for the night. The sun was just beginning to set, and he wanted to have a good sleep so he could enjoy the next day.

'Oh yes', he chuckled to himself, 'the sun is not

only brightest at noonday, but hottest too. I am going to have fun with Emu'.

Towards noon the next day all the bush creatures gathered at the billabong to see who would win this unusual challenge. Emu hadn't had such a large audience for ages. He pranced, preened and strutted through the crowd. Now and then he spread out his extraordinary wings for show. And in moments of silence he burst into song about himself.

'Poor Kookaburra', sighed Kangaroo, who was the official starter. 'He hasn't got a chance. I almost wish he could win, just to teach Emu a lesson.'

When the sun stood directly over the tallest tree on a nearby hill, Emu knew it was time to begin.

He turned to Kookaburra and said unpleasantly, 'If I were you I'd never fly again after I'm done!'

'After you're done . . .' retorted Kookaburra, but his voice trailed away. He wanted to say, 'You'll be done, all right – well done!' But he didn't. Instead he hung his head and feigned sadness.

'Just ignore him, Kookaburra', said Wombat, who was a friendly creature.

Emu raised one big foot over Wombat, who quickly scurried away.

'Are you ready, Emu?' asked Kangaroo.

'Of course I am!'

'Right, stand back everyone', commanded Kangaroo.

Emu strutted to the starting line.

'On your mark.'

Emu dug in his claws and leant forward.

'Get ready.'

Emu breathed deeply and puffed out his chest.

'Go!'

Emu was off, taking great strides down past the billabong and into a clearing. His huge wings spread out, his feet and legs disappeared under him, and he was away.

Soon he was no more than a small, dark speck on the wide horizon. A speck that gradually grew smaller and smaller as it moved towards the sun. It wasn't long before he'd disappeared completely. 'Ooh!' they all gasped when a small, bright red ball suddenly exploded and shot out from the surface of the sun.

'What's happening?' asked Wombat.

No one bothered to reply. They were all too busy running for cover as the flaming crimson ball grew larger and larger and plummeted towards Earth.

The whistling sound the ball made grew louder and louder until suddenly there was a huge splash. The ball had landed in the billabong. Steam hissed and billowed everywhere. Once the bush creatures had stopped coughing they all began to creep out from behind their separate hiding places. Kangaroo bravely led the way back to the billabong.

'Argh!' they all screamed in horror when a strange-looking head on a long, thin neck popped up out of the water.

'Is . . . is . . . is that you, Emu?' asked Wombat nervously. Then he began to chuckle at what he thought was his foolishness. Of course it wasn't Emu. Emu didn't look anything like that.

But Kookaburra, realising what had happened, began to laugh and laugh.

The mud-coloured monster with the strange head and long neck stood up, shook himself and walked from the water. He glared disgustedly at Kookaburra, who was practically hysterical, and said, 'Yes, it is me. I am Emu'.

There was stunned silence.

'But where are your beautiful feathers?' croaked Frog.

'Burnt', choked Emu.

'What about your wings?'

'They exploded when I reached the sun. All I have left now are these small, brown stumps. I don't think I will be able to fly any more. It looks like you've got the last laugh after all, Kookaburra', finished Emu tearfully.

Everyone looked accusingly at Kookaburra. Emu had been terribly vain, but he didn't deserve this.

Kookaburra didn't feel the tiniest bit guilty. He congratulated himself on having the last laugh as he flew off into the bush cackling, 'Kook, kook, koo, kaa, kaa, haa, haa, haa . . .'

When the water in the billabong finally settled and Emu was able to have a good look at his new appearance, he was so embarrassed that he ran away as fast as his legs could carry him.

For days and days he ran. For weeks and weeks he ran. He ran so much that he became very, very good at it. Soon he was the fastest-running bird in Australia. And it wasn't long before he was singing a new song:

> I love my great big feet!
> I love my strong, fast legs!
> I run so fast, you eat my dust,
> I'm the fastest bird around!

# Old poker face

Before time began, the Good Spirit was sitting thinking about what he could make. 'Things of beauty', he said to himself, 'with plenty of brilliant colour. Different shapes, sizes and textures. Funny things to make me laugh. And yes, mysterious things so that when I make people and animals they will have something to think about'.

The Good Spirit chuckled. There was nothing he loved more than making something new. He rubbed his hands together eagerly and with great gusto hurled a sun into being. 'Aah, that's better', he said. 'Now I can see what I'm doing.'

After that he created many planets, and they all beamed at one another, happy to be in existence.

The Good Spirit was really beginning to enjoy himself as were all his new creations. 'More, more, make more of us', they chorused. They couldn't wait to see what he would do next.

'Hmmmnnn', murmured the Good Spirit in reply. 'You are all beautiful and interesting, but none of you have mystery.' The planets looked at themselves and had to admit this was true. They felt sad.

Sun sighed deeply, but comforted himself with his obvious beauty. Then he had a bright idea. 'Good Spirit', he said warmly, 'you can make any-thing. Please make something mysterious so we can all experience it'.

Everyone shouted their approval.

'Quiet now', their maker chuckled. 'I will create something mysterious to hover with you, but let me think about it first.'

This made them so excited they rolled around making a terrible racket.

'Settle down, settle down', laughed the Good Spirit. 'How can I concentrate when you're all being silly?'

They quickly and quietly rolled back to their places in space and gave him time to think.

'A little music, please', said the Good Spirit

after some time. They all began to hum slowly.

Suddenly, with a great swoop of his hand, he flung into space a thing so mysterious that everyone was too stunned even to gasp.

'What is it? What is it?' they finally murmured as they stared at the pale, round, lumpy object hovering near them.

'Moon', replied its maker.

'Moon', they echoed. 'Moo-oon, moo-oon.' On and on they chanted until finally the Good Spirit said, 'Let's talk to Moon'. The planets all fell silent. They felt nervous about speaking to Moon. Surely something so mysterious must have very important things to say.

'How are you, Moon?' enquired the Good Spirit kindly.

'I'd rather not have a name, thank you', replied Moon very seriously.

'Don't you like your name?'

'It's not a question of like or dislike. I'm here to be a mystery.'

Everyone was stunned to think that Moon would dare to speak to the Good Spirit like that.

Fortunately, the Good Spirit was in a happy mood.

'You're a cheeky one', he said as he tickled Moon's chin.

'I won't laugh!' replied Moon. 'I'm the mysterious one. I don't want to smile.'

'Well, what do you want to do?' asked his maker.

'I want to fascinate', replied Moon. 'I want to fascinate everything!'

'Oh dear', sighed the Good Spirit. 'Oh dear, oh dear. We can't have that, it will only lead to harm. All my creatures will be mesmerised by you, and they won't be able to go about their business. I must find a way to help you fit in with the rest of the world.'

The others hovered silently, sensing their maker's sorrow. They were very angry with Moon and were secretly hoping the Good Spirit would get rid of him. Then they wouldn't have to put up with the old poker face.

Sighing again, the Good Spirit turned and once more stretched out his huge hand. He hurled into being the most beautiful planet they had ever seen. It was full of bright blues and greens. It was a great triumph. They all clapped and cheered. All except Moon, who was too busy looking mysterious to even notice.

'Earth', the Good Spirit said to the new planet, 'you will keep Moon in line, for whether old poker face likes it or not he will look down on you and smile, and with each smile his fascination will lessen'.

'Not fair! Not fair!' called Moon keeping up his poker face more than ever. 'You can't make me smile. I will never smile!'

But just then the shadow of Earth passed glee-fully across Moon's face and he was left with a giant grin.

The Good Spirit and all the others laughed and laughed.

# The laziest seagull

The Lazy Seagull was the laziest seagull in the world. She was so lazy that she dropped her eggs as she flew along instead of laying them in a nest. The kangaroos never looked up when the Lazy Seagull was around. They knew that if they did they might end up with two fat egg yolks over their eyes. Of course, none of the snakes complained. They loved eggs, cracked or whole, but the other birds were very embarrassed by her. When they were busy nest building, the Lazy Seagull would swoop down and try to persuade them to leave their work and play with her.

'Come and fly, come and have fun', she would say. Play, not work, was the Lazy Seagull's motto.

'Go away', the other birds would answer crossly. 'We're nesting!'

'I never nest', she would reply.

One day Pelican decided to test the Lazy Seagull.

'We know you never nest', said Pelican. 'You leave mess everywhere. You should have been born a cloud, you love the sky so much.'

'I can nest', said the Lazy Seagull, whose pride was offended. 'I just choose not to.'

'You wouldn't know a nest if you fell over one', said Heron.

'SQUAWK!' cried the Lazy Seagull angrily. 'Of course I would!'

Pelican threw back his head and laughed. 'You see this fat, tender fish in my bill?' he asked the Lazy Seagull.

'Oooh, yes', she replied as she peered in. She'd love to pinch it.

'I'll give it to you', Pelican said generously, 'if you lay your eggs in a nest'.

The Lazy Seagull didn't want to build a nest, but she did want the fish so she agreed.

'You'll have to show me the nest', warned Pelican. 'And not one egg can be broken.'

The Lazy Seagull flew off with her stomach

rumbling to look for twigs and bits of seaweed. She collected some odds and ends and placed them on a large, flat rock near the water.

'I think a nest is round', she muttered as she walked in circles dragging the seaweed behind her. She spent the best part of the morning trying to build a nest but the seaweed slipped away and the twigs rolled off one another.

'SQUAWK! SQUAWK! SQUAWK!' she screeched in anger. 'I hate building nests!'

And she flew off to find one to steal.

As she glided over a swampy beach she saw Little Turtle sunning himself on the sand. His shell is round like a nest, she thought. I wonder if he'd give it to me? She swooped down and landed next to him.

'What a lovely shell you have, Little Turtle', she said smoothly.

'Why, thank you', he said, blushing.

'It's not as beautiful as your skin though', she sighed.

'Really?' asked Little Turtle, who was secretly ashamed of his wrinkly skin.

'Really', answered the Lazy Seagull.

Little Turtle looked down at his front legs and decided they didn't seem nearly as wrinkled as they had a moment ago.

After a while the Lazy Seagull sighed, 'It's a pity about your shell, isn't it?'

'Why?' he asked in surprise.

'Your mother hasn't told you, has she?' said the Lazy Seagull shaking her head.

'Told me what?'

'Told you that turtles used to be famous for the silky, smooth skin on their backs.'

'How do you know?'

'How do I know? Goodness, I'm no ordinary bird! I might look young, but I'm really very, very old. I was alive when turtles were free of those things', she said pointing to his shell.

'Why do we have them then?' he asked.

'Why? Because of Magic Owl, of course! He was very beautiful and very good at magic. He out-shone everyone until turtles came along. You see, turtles were not only handsome, but fast runners too. Owl was jealous of their speed as well as their soft, fine skin. He cast a magic spell on all turtles, making them carry a shell that covered their beautiful skin and made them move very, very slowly.'

'I knew it!' said Little Turtle. 'I knew I was meant to be handsome! How fast could we run before we had shells?'

'As fast as an emu.'

'It's not fair!' he cried. 'Why did this have to happen to us?'

'Poor Little Turtle', cooed the Lazy Seagull. 'Don't you know that Magic Owl has been dead for a long time now? Owls these days have no magic at all. Why don't you take that awful shell off and I'll get rid of it for you?'

Little Turtle happily slipped out of his shell and pushed it towards the Lazy Seagull.

'I don't feel any faster', he said, shivering.

'That's because your shell has been squashing your legs', answered the Lazy Seagull quickly. 'Soon they'll grow long and strong and you'll be able to run as fast as the wind.'

'Oh thank you, Seagull', he called as she dragged his shell down the beach.

When Mother Turtle returned to find her son naked and sunburnt she was very cross.

'Who told you you could remove your shell?' she asked.

'My friend, Seagull', he replied. And he told her the whole sorry story.

'You silly little fool', she scolded. 'A turtle's pride is in his shell, not his skin. Now get into the water before you become roast turtle. I'll go and look for your shell.'

The Lazy Seagull was laying her eggs when Mother Turtle came by.

'Good morning, Seagull', Mother Turtle called. She pretended not to notice the shell.

'Morning', said Lazy Seagull grumpily.

'Beautiful day for flying', sighed Mother Turtle as she looked up at the clear, blue sky. 'You know, Seagull, the sea is to me as the sky is to you. Fun, fun and more fun!'

'Ooh, yes', said the Lazy Seagull, who suddenly had a deep longing to soar as high and fast as she could.

'Poor Seagull', said Mother Turtle. 'Why don't you let me bring your nest down from that great, big, shadowy rock? If you leave it on the beach the sun will keep your eggs warm. And I'll stand guard for snakes. You're too young to be doing all this work.'

The Lazy Seagull was so keen to be off she didn't stop to realise it was a trick.

'Oh, thank you!' she said happily and within seconds she was soaring high in the sky. I'd better bring Pelican back, then I can have that juicy, tender fish and be rid of those eggs for good, she thought as she glided with the wind. She was very hungry after all that work and very cross for having to nest in the first place.

Mother Turtle raised her heavy body up onto the large rock. Then she reached out her front leg and gently knocked the shell down. The eggs fell out and rolled into a hollow in the sand. Some lucky snake is going to enjoy those, she thought as she dragged the shell back to her son.

'Let that be a lesson to you', she growled when she finally reached him. 'Use your brains when someone tells you a story, and don't believe every word that's said.'

Little Turtle grinned sheepishly and slipped his handsome shell back on.

Soon the Lazy Seagull and Pelican were circling overhead. The Lazy Seagull looked in vain for the nest.

'The only things I can see', said Pelican, 'are two turtles making for the swamp and a snake on the beach with a contented look on his face'.

'What!' screeched the Lazy Seagull as she swooped down. The happy snake burped and slithered off. The Lazy Seagull followed, squawking and pecking it angrily.

The Lazy Seagull turned with dismay when she heard a long 'gulp'. Pelican grinned, 'That was one delicious fish! What a pity you missed out on it, Seagull'.

'SQUAWK! SQUAWK! SQUAWK!' The Lazy Seagull screeched as she flew at him. Pelican just laughed and flew off, leaving the hungry, angry Lazy Seagull to spend the rest of the day scavenging for food and thinking about her idle ways.

# Jilji and the magic bird

There was a time long ago when only human beings could see. All other living things were left in the dark. Australia was filled with the moans and groans and oohs and aahs of bruised animals, birds and reptiles. Kangaroos were constantly apologising for landing on other, smaller bush creatures. The poor old wombats were often half squashed. Emus were always angry with koalas for mistaking emu legs for tree trunks. And echidnas were forever stabbing others in the back with their quills. As you can imagine, it was a very dangerous time in which to be an animal.

Most people treated the blind bush creatures kindly. However, there was a man called Fatfella who was particularly horrible. If you met him on a dark, stormy night you'd think he was a monster. He was short and very, very wide with small, beady eyes that glinted evilly in the dark. In the moonlight, his eyes changed colour from brown to yellow, and his teeth took on a reddish tinge – the colour of blood. No one could be blamed for wondering if he was human or not!

Fatfella had two hobbies: killing and eating. There was nothing he loved more than walking through the bush whacking things on the head with his big, heavy wokkaburra. The more he killed the more he ate. And the more he ate the larger his stomach grew, so the hungrier he became. It was a vicious circle. Eventually, he became so fat that his brain began to go silly.

It's just amazing what idiotic thoughts passed through Fatfella's addled brain. He began to think he was extremely clever and better than everyone else. He started eating crocodiles to make his teeth bigger and sharper. Then he went on to owls, believing they would increase his already enormous brainpower. After that he hunted kangaroos in the ridiculous belief that he would be able to jump higher. All in all, he was a pretty strange character. If he were alive today we'd probably say he was off the planet.

One day, a plucky little girl called Jilji saw Fatfella chewing on a spiky echidna and, from a safe distance, she called out, 'Hey Fatfella, you're going to have very sharp hair if you don't watch out!'

This made him so cross that he choked on a quill and vomited all he'd eaten. He went purple with rage and swore revenge. This wasn't the first time Jilji had taunted him. He was sick of her making smart comments about his eating habits.

Now, you would think that anyone with a brain larger than a pea would agree with Jilji. But many didn't. In fact, there were a surprising number of people who actually worshipped Fatfella. Jilji's uncle, Wanya, had nicknamed them 'Fatfella's mob'. Wanya thought they were awful because they amused themselves day and night by playing horrid, nasty tricks on anything unlucky enough to get in their way. Jilji agreed wholeheartedly with Wanya.

The mob liked to shove small goannas under kangaroos as they were about to land so they'd be squashed flat. Besides this thoroughly dreadful practice, they delighted in holding up thick pieces of wood so the poor, blind birds would fly into them and knock themselves silly. They tied snakes around rocks and threw them into the river, and flattened every insect they saw. And all the time they were being mean and horrible they chanted a silly, little song:

> Fatfella, Fatfella,
> We're his fans.
> Fatfella, Fatfella,
> He's our man!

Fatfella and his band of followers held meetings at night to plan their more elaborate tricks. And just to be spiteful, they held these evil gatherings on the banks of the sacred water-hole of Kagara, the giant striped snake of ancient legends. The keeper of the sacred water-hole was Wanya, Jilji's uncle. Wanya was deeply offended by the mob's use of such a sacred place, but he was old and there was little he could do except tell them off now and then. They just jeered at his stories of Kagara.

At the sacred water-hole Fatfella and his mob always built huge bonfires and gorged themselves on damper, vegetables and any creatures they'd killed. They even chewed the bones, grinding them to a fine powder with their already over-worked teeth. Any gristly bits they spat into Kagara's water-hole. When all the food was gone they competed with one another to see who could come up with the dirtiest deed. But, so far, no one had been able to beat Fatfella, who was a master of the art of being totally disgusting.

Now, Kagara's water-hole was reputed to be a place of very powerful magic, but Fatfella and his mob weren't frightened of anything.

'If Kagara ever surfaces I'll eat him!' boasted Fatfella one night. 'He doesn't scare me!'

'Yeah!' his fans chorused. 'We'll tie him around a big rock and throw him in the river like we did with the other slimy snakes!'

Unbeknown to the mob, Jilji and her uncle Wanya were keeping watch from the cover of nearby bushes.

'They're all so bloated with their own import-ance', Wanya whispered to Jilji as he watched them feasting. 'They've forgotten just how danger-ous Kagara can be. They'll pay for this one day.'

They crouched lower among the bushes as Fatfella suddenly sprang up and shouted loudly:

> Fatfella, Fatfella,
> Big hunting man!
> Fatfella, Fatfella,
> Greatest in the land!

Fatfella then stood with his legs apart and beat his chest hard with his fist until every blubbery layer on his body wobbled like a fat wombat's backside.

'I've got crocodile teeth', he said as he bared his blood-coloured teeth and ran around his circle of fans, spitting and snarling. They all cheered.

'And I've got kangaroo legs!' he screeched as he began to jump all over the place.

He stopped and stared at his spellbound audience.

'I'm wise like an owl', he moaned softly in a voice as scary as death.

Then he held his hands to his head and made his eyes bulge so that they looked like yellow saucers in the moonlight.

'What a feather-brain!' whispered Jilji.

'Don't talk like that around Fatfella', Wanya warned her, for he knew how cheeky she could be. 'If you get into trouble with him, I doubt that I will be able to help you.'

Jilji reluctantly agreed to hold her tongue, but she knew it would be difficult. She was too much like her uncle.

'I'll show you all how brave and clever I am', Fatfella was saying now. 'I'll swim down to the bottom of the water-hole and eat Kagara!' For a tiny moment there was complete silence. Perhaps some of them were remembering the stories they'd been told as children about Kagara's power. Then the moment passed, and they were all clapping and cheering and urging him on.

'We must stop him', Wanya said to Jilji. 'He'll cause great harm.'

But it was too late. Fatfella had already leapt into the water-hole and disappeared.

The old man and his niece watched fearfully,

not sure what would happen, until Fatfella finally emerged puffing, panting and burping.

'He wasn't that big', he boasted as he heaved himself out onto the rocks. 'He was just an ordinary giant snake, and very tasty too!'

The mob cheered wildly.

'Did he really eat Kagara?' asked Jilji tearfully.

'No', said Wanya. 'He's full of nothing but hot air and silly tricks. It would serve him right if someone ate him though!'

The following day strange things began to happen. The water-hole dried out. By sunset all that was left was a tiny pool way down deep among the rocks at the bottom of the hole.

The mob gathered together, talking noisily about the strange event. Fatfella was convinced that it was all due to his power. I am invincible, he thought vainly. No one can beat me: neither man nor spirit! He decided he wanted everyone, not just the blind animals, to be under his power. He ordered the group to be silent while he tried to work out how he was going to achieve this.

Fatfella remembered the poisonous Yamilli creeper, which he'd been warned not to touch as a boy. He smiled a cruel, evil smile. The creeper was just what he needed.

Soon the fans were collecting as much as they could find. They dried the leaves in the sun and then ground them into a fine powder and mixed it with water into a purplish liquid. When the work was finished Fatfella passed around gumnuts of poison to the mob.

'Blind all those people who won't agree to me being boss. They won't be any trouble after that. Be careful though', he warned them. 'One drop will blind but two will kill. Remember I want living subjects, not dead ones. And leave Jilji to me. I have a better plan for that brat!'

'But can we tie that uncle of hers around a rock and throw him into the river?' someone asked eagerly.

'A wonderful suggestion', replied Fatfella. 'But not yet. I want to see Wanya suffer from the poison first.'

It wasn't long before nearly everyone was blind except the mob. Those who still had their sight had kept it only by agreeing to be slaves. Wanya was the first to be blinded, and poor Jilji had to promise to be Fatfella's personal cook to stop Fatfella from drowning her uncle in the river.

Jilji worked day and night, but no matter how hard she tried she just couldn't do anything right. Fatfella loved picking on her and making her cry. For the sake of her old uncle, she always had to bite back her defiant retorts. While he was alive, there was nothing else she could do.

One day, after Fatfella had held Wanya over the river to punish Jilji for serving up tough meat, she escaped to what was left of Kagara's waterhole, and cried and cried.

'Why are you crying?' a voice asked when her sobs had died down.

'Who's there?' she asked, not lifting her head from her arms.

'It'sss me', the voice replied.

Jilji looked up and saw a small bird with striped feathers standing next to her. 'Birds can't talk', she said impatiently.

'I jussst did', he replied.

'Oh, why don't you go away and leave me alone!' she said tearfully.

'Are you alwaysss thisss cheerful?' asked the bird cheekily as he fluttered his big eyes at her.

'Hey, you're not like all the other bush creatures! You can see', she exclaimed, looking more closely at the Magic Bird. 'Not that it matters', she sighed gloomily. 'Seeing makes no difference around here any more. If you hang around they'll chop you up into little pieces and make me cook you on the fire. You'd better go.'

'But I have nowhere to go', he said. 'It looksss as though you'll have to take care of me. Maybe one day I'll be able to help you.'

'No one can help me', she said despairingly. 'And if Fatfella sees you he'll eat you straight away. He's never eaten a talking bird before.'

'Why don't you hide me in your dillybag', suggested the Magic Bird as he hopped closer. 'I'm sssure your family would love me. Don't they need sssomeone to cheer them up?'

For the first time in weeks Jilji smiled. 'What a strange creature you are', she said. 'All right, we'll see how things go.' She opened her bag and the Magic Bird hopped in.

The Magic Bird was right, Jilji's family loved him. Especially blind Wanya, who said he was a sign that things would change for the better. However, such an unusual bird couldn't remain a secret for long. One person told another, always in secret of course, until, inevitably, the story reached the fat ears of Fatfella himself.

'A talking, seeing bird', he repeated over and over when he heard. 'It must be a magic bird. If I ate it I could do magic too . . . Bring Jilji to me!' he roared.

The mob dragged Jilji up to where Fatfella stood. Fatfella waved his podgy hand and they shoved her to the ground.

'Where's that bird of yours?' he demanded.

Jilji said nothing. She loved the Magic Bird as deeply as her uncle did. They'd both rather die than betray such a special creature.

Fatfella continued to demand that she tell him, but to no avail. He pushed his great, bulging face up close to hers and shouted, 'WHERE'S THE BIRD?'

'You smell like rotting meat', Jilji said. She'd had enough. She'd decided that if these were to be her last moments she might as well enjoy them.

Fatfella swelled up with anger and screamed with rage. 'You insulting, horrible child! Tell me or I'll eat you instead!'

Jilji gulped in horror. She hadn't anticipated such a grisly end. She'd rather be anything than yet another roll of fat around Fatfella's stomach. But she swallowed her fear and shouted defiantly, 'Maggot mouth! I'll never tell you. NEVER!'

Fatfella raised his wokkaburra, but just then a voice said, 'Looking for me, fatssso?'

Fatfella swung around and saw the Magic Bird.

'ARGH!' Fatfella screamed and went racing towards him.

The Magic Bird fluttered quickly to one side, causing Fatfella to land with an awful thud on his big belly.

'Get me up!' he squealed, wriggling his porky legs helplessly in the air. His fans rolled him over, and he shouted at them to get the Magic Bird.

Straight away spears, boomerangs and wokka-burras went flying through the air, but, for some strange reason, they missed the bird and returned to attack the throwers instead. The Magic Bird watched with glee as they all began fighting one another.

Fatfella went beserk. 'Fight the bird, not each other', he cried. 'Look, there he is, hovering above you. Chase him!'

'You'll never catch me you sssilly foolsss!' the bird cried as he flew off in the direction of the sacred water-hole.

Fatfella ran after him, frenzied by the thought of how powerful he would be if he could only eat that bird. All his fans followed thinking they'd like a piece of the Magic Bird too. When the Magic Bird reached the water-hole he flew down among the rocks that lined it and disappeared. His pursuers were so crazy to catch him that they leapt into the water-hole and slid down to the bottom. They searched and searched for the Magic Bird but there was no sign of him. Suddenly a hole opened up between the two largest, lowest rocks in the water-hole and they dived through, thinking the Magic Bird was hiding in there.

The hole, which was really the mouth of Kagara, snapped shut after the last fan had entered. When the snake opened his mouth again, they'd all disappeared from view.

Kagara smiled and burped. 'What a horrible tassste', he said. Then he curled up and went to sleep. As he slept the water began to return to its natural level. At the same time all the people who had been blinded by the poison received their sight back. Stranger still, the blind bush creatures could now see. They blinked painfully as the sun dazzled their eyes, but they were soon hopping, jumping, flying and slithering all over the place.

That night Jilji dreamt about the Magic Bird. It was a wonderful dream in which he flew down and hovered over her and said, 'It'sss me!'

'Yesss, I know', she giggled. 'Hello, Kagara!'

# The night sky

When the Good Spirit hurled the planet Earth into being, everything on it was one big, gloomy muddle. There were big shapes, little shapes and long and skinny shapes all worming and squirming and bumping around, and to make matters worse they were all joined together. It was impossible to tell where a monster ended and a rock began, or a tree started and a river finished.

The Good Spirit spent years trying to sort out the muddle, but when he finally got the trees untangled from the rivers, the monsters off the rocks and the children separated from the wombats, the confusion multiplied. Trees talked nineteen to the dozen, rivers overflowed and wet everything, rocks rolled around squashing things, and monsters howled in pain as they ate themselves. The Good Spirit rolled his eyes and prayed for patience. He was so tired after all his work that he decided the mess could sort itself out, and he went to sleep for a couple of hundred years.

It was a long time before everything did get sorted out on Earth. Trees, who'd always had a mind of their own, suddenly stopped talking. They grew tall and thin, short and fat, or twisted and curly. The rivers became smoother and quieter, but they remained bad tempered and overflowed when anyone upset them. Rocks grew fat and heavy and stubborn, and only moved when they had to. Monsters stopped eating themselves and roamed around at night looking for people to devour instead.

One night, when the Good Spirit was enjoying his deeply peaceful sleep a very irritating whining noise suddenly woke him up.

'Wh . . . wh . . . what was that?' he muttered as he reluctantly rubbed the sleep from his eyes.

'I hate the dark!' shouted a boy's voice from Earth. 'I hate it! I hate it! I hate it!'

'Hmph', muttered the Good Spirit as he opened his eyes wide and peered down. 'Nothing wrong with a bit of darkness. Couldn't sleep without it, myself. Besides, there's Moon for night-time.'

'Now, now, Moonga', the boy's mother soothed, unaware that the Good Spirit was listening. 'You go to sleep and I'll watch over you.'

'No fear', replied Moonga. 'If you drop off we'll both be dinner!'

It was all very well for the Good Spirit to have left everything on Earth to sort itself out while he was safely asleep in the clouds, but Earth had become a very frightening place for people and animals because of all the meat-eating monsters. After sunset the monsters gathered together, licking their lips and making horrible, disgusting noises; the dark night was the easiest time to catch humans. Moon made a very dim effort to provide light to Earth, and the Good Spirit hadn't yet got around to creating anything else to help after Sun went down. No one slept well because people who fell into a deep sleep usually failed to wake up when a monster rumbled up to eat them. No wonder Moonga was frightened of the dark!

'It's so unfair, Mother', he whined. 'I'd love to be able to sleep well. I'd love to be a dreamer. I'm sure I was born to be one. But I don't want to be monster bait.'

'Well, well, well', said the Good Spirit, who was still eavesdropping. 'And I thought children were meant to play. You learn something new every day.'

Meanwhile Moonga's mother was saying, 'I'm sure the Good Spirit will hear our complaints and do something about them.'

'I don't think the Good Spirit listens to us at all', Moonga said crossly. 'I think you're wrong, Mother. I bet all he does is sleep.'

'Of course he listens.'

'Well, I've been yelling for a long time and he hasn't listened to me yet. If it wasn't for Moon I wouldn't even be able to see my own hand at night. If he doesn't give us more light soon I'm going to make a huge ladder and climb up and tear holes in the night sky!'

'You mustn't even think of such a thing', cautioned his mother. 'You know what they say: the clouds in the night sky are the Good Spirit's blanket. Without the cloud blanket he couldn't sleep.'

'Oh, great!' retorted Moonga angrily. 'So while he's all snuggly and warm we get eaten!'

The Good Spirit yawned. 'Honestly! The boy has no patience. I hope he sees the light soon. In the meantime I'll have to keep an eye on him now and then I suppose.' And he snuggled down under his blanket and went back to sleep.

In the end Moonga decided action was better than words. He gathered strong sticks from the bush and tied them together with vines to make a ladder. Day after day he worked until his ladder seemed to go on forever. However, to Moonga's bewilderment, the longer his ladder grew, the further away the clouds and the sky appeared.

'If I didn't know better', he finally said to himself, 'I'd swear that sky keeps moving'.

After months of hard work, Moonga gave up in despair. It seemed it didn't matter how many sticks he joined together, his ladder would never be long enough.

'Darn', said the Good Spirit. 'He's given up. And I was having such fun'. He pushed the sky back to where it had always been.

By this time, the Good Spirit had developed a personal interest in Moonga. The next time he looked down to see what the boy was up to, he found him collecting feathers and bark.

'I'm sure I'll be able to fly once I've made my wings', Moonga said confidently to himself. 'I'm going to get to that old spirit's cloud blanket one way or another.'

'Oh good', chuckled the Good Spirit. 'He hasn't given up after all.'

As Moonga stuffed more and more feathers into his dillybag they began to poke through and tickle his side. Moonga was a very ticklish boy, and he began to laugh and laugh. He laughed so much that the Good Spirit couldn't help joining in. While Moonga giggled uncontrollably, the Good Spirit positively roared with hysteria. Soon tears were flooding down his cheeks and wetting the universe.

Moonga quickly crawled under a thick bush to shelter from what he thought was rain. 'How strange', he said as he peered out from under the leaves. 'There's not a cloud in the sky.'

The next time the Good Spirit looked for Moonga, he discovered him perched on the top of a cliff. Moonga had two huge bark wings strapped to his back, with feathers glued all over them, and a sharp shell beak fastened over his mouth.

The Good Spirit clapped enthusiastically. He loved a good spectacle. The noise caused Moonga to look up at the thundering sky. He hoped it wouldn't rain again.

Moonga stretched out his arms and bravely said, 'I, Moonga the Magnificent, will now practise flying. Then tonight I will fly away from the monsters, up and up until I reach the cloud blanket. With my fine beak I will peck holes all over it'. He spoke very loudly to give himself confidence. Really he was scared stiff.

'I don't know about this', muttered the Good Spirit as he scrunched up his blanket and hid it behind him. 'I think the boy's going too far.'

The Good Spirit watched as Moonga threw himself off the cliff.

'ARRRRRGGH!' Moonga screamed as he fell down, down, down towards the rocky ground below.

A nearby river moved slightly and he landed in it.

His screams brought his mother rushing down to the river bank. She dragged him from the water, growling, 'You silly child! You're a boy, not a bird!'

'I wish he was a bird', yawned the Good Spirit. 'Then I wouldn't have had to move that river for him. Birds are lovely; they're happy just laying those little round things. They don't want to dream. Oh well, I suppose the show's over for today.' He pulled his old cloud blanket out from behind him and gave it an affectionate cuddle.

'I don't know why that boy wants to dream', he sighed as he curled up to go back to sleep. 'Dreaming is a terrible business. I dream every night, and in the morning I find all these things that I don't remember making. After all, I didn't really plan to make those monsters the boy is always complaining about.' The Good Spirit closed his eyes and began to snore.

'It sounds like there's going to be a storm tonight', Moonga said as he cuddled up to his mother.

'Maybe not', she replied. 'It keeps stopping and starting.'

A small planet was suddenly sucked into the Good Spirit's left nostril. He snorted loudly and it shot out again.

'I think that's the last of it', said Moonga's mother. 'Try and sleep now.'

Moonga was very, very tired that night. He was tired of worrying about being eaten by the monsters, tired of wishing he could dream, and tired of planning new ways to reach that stupid cloud blanket. Perhaps it was because he was so tired that, for the first time in his life, he dreamt.

In his dream he was flying, but without wings. He soared through the dark sky, going higher and higher and faster and faster. He came to a halt when his head bumped against the cloud blanket. Moonga reached out his hand and touched it. It was soft and bumpy – just how he imagined a cloud would feel. Moonga continued to feel the cloud. The slumbering Good Spirit wrapped inside began to feel a little ticklish.

Moonga pushed his whole hand into the cloud mass and was dazzled when a star-shaped beam of light shone through. He was so excited with this success that he made more holes. And soon there were stars all over the place.

In his own dream, the Good Spirit was wriggling uncomfortably.

Moonga became very adventurous and pushed not only his hand but his whole body up through the cloud blanket. Before he knew it he was sitting on a rather enormous heavenly stomach. He turned around and closed the large gap he had made. Then he slowly crawled up to the Good Spirit's head.

He sat on the Good Spirit's chest and looked at him crossly. The Good Spirit had a smile on his face as he slept and that made Moonga even angrier. He leant forward and, with both hands, pinched the Good Spirit's very large nostrils.

The Good Spirit opened one eye.

'BOO!' shouted Moonga. 'I've made stars to help light up the night sky so that we can feel safe for once.'

'And a draught', shivered the Good Spirit. 'That's the trouble with making things. You often get two for the price of one.'

'Promise you won't unmake them?' asked Moonga determinedly.

'I never unmake', yawned the Good Spirit. 'I just keep trying new things.'

'I can dream like you now', Moonga said boldly.

'Heaven help us', sighed the Good Spirit. 'A word of advice, then. Never dream to finish, only to begin.'

'But you dream to finish', protested Moonga. 'Sun is finished and that planet, and . . . and Moon is definitely complete.'

'Aah', the Good Spirit replied, 'but what about the rivers on Earth? You've seen *them* change, haven't you?'

'Well', said Moonga confidently, 'I know one thing that *is* finished – me!'

The Good Spirit laughed loudly. 'You only think you're finished', he chuckled. 'None of the things you see here are finished, not one. And that includes you. Things are always evolving and changing and balancing out. Nothing ever stays the same. That gives you something to think about, doesn't it?'

With a laugh the Good Spirit picked up Moonga and dropped him gently over the cloud blanket. As he floated towards Earth, Moonga began to grow sleepier and sleepier. Just as he was drifting off he heard the Good Spirit say, 'Who knows, Moonga, I might give you wings one day.'

When Moonga woke up it was raining. He rubbed his wet eyes and rolled away from his mother. If only he could have dreams like that every night, he thought as he stretched and yawned. Suddenly, he realised that although it was still night-time, it wasn't pitch black any more. He looked up and, to his amazement, saw the stars that he'd made in his dream. Moon smiled down at him and the stars winked merrily. For the first time in his life the night sky seemed friendly and helpful.

'Yippee!' he yelled as he leapt into the air. 'Yahoo!'

As if in response to his shouting there was a low rumble of thunder, and Moonga had the strangest feeling that it actually said, 'My good-ness it's cold up here. I need another sun . . .'

# The vibs

Yutta was a VIB, a Very Important Bird. He'd invented the VIBC, the Very Important Bird Club, a very exclusive organisation.

You could tell VIBs by the way they walked or, rather, strutted – legs fully extended, head high and tail back. Also, VIBs looked at other birds in a way that made them immediately check to see if their feathers were clean. The VIBs had very high opinions of themselves and very low opinions of others. And just why were VIBs so special? Because they belonged to the VIBC, of course!

Now, not all of the other birds wanted to be VIBs. Some thought the whole thing was silly, especially considering you had to wear a kangaroo paw flower on the top of your head when you attended a meeting. Even so, there were quite a large number of birds who would do anything to belong to the VIBC and who didn't mind the idea of strutting around with a flower on their heads.

Nindi was a young bird who had wanted to be a VIB for as long as he could remember. From the day he'd first learnt to walk he'd been practising his strutting. And he often perched a piece of kangaroo paw on his head to make himself look grander. His friend Tilla, who was older and wiser, looked on the club as nothing short of ridiculous, but she refrained from saying so. Nindi was very young and with any luck he'd grow out of it.

'If you learn to strut, too, we can both join', Nindi told Tilla one lazy afternoon. Tilla yawned contentedly. She was quite happy with her life the way it was.

'I'd give my right leg to be a VIB', continued Nindi as he strutted back and forth. 'They're such important birds!'

Tilla smiled to herself. There was no way Nindi would be able to strut with only one leg!

'Who says they're important?' she asked.

'They do!' said Nindi innocently.

'Exactly!'

Nindi was convinced that his friend Tilla was just pretending she didn't want to join, so he ignored her and went on practising.

Now, there's one thing you should know about VIBs: they had fun mostly by making fun of others. In fact, they'd been known to go out of their way to find trusting birds like Nindi, and talk them into doing all sorts of strange things. Their leader, Yutta, had for some time been watching Nindi practising his strutting, and he'd decided that the little bird could give the members of the VIBC a great deal of amusement.

'Your strutting's improved', he said slyly to Nindi one day.

'Really?' asked Nindi, blushing with pleasure.

'Perhaps it's time we put you through the VIBCI', suggested Yutta importantly.

'What's that?'

'The Very Important Bird Club Initiation, of course!'

'Of course!' said Nindi, who didn't want to appear ignorant. 'And after that will I be a VIB?'

'Ye-es . . . if you pass.'

'I'll pass, I'll do anything!' said the little bird excitedly.

How touching, thought Yutta, who was already thinking of all sorts of weird and wonderful things he could get Nindi to do.

Tilla was most unimpressed by Nindi's good news.

'Secret initiation, eh?' she said pessimistically. 'More like stupid initiation! You don't need to be a VIB, Nindi. You're a good bird just as you are.'

'But I'm not important!'

'Neither are they!'

'Yes they are and I want to be the same!'

'Please yourself', sighed Tilla when she saw how determined Nindi was. 'Just don't forget who your real friends are!'

'Once I'm a VIB everyone will be my friend.'

Tilla closed her eyes and pretended she was asleep. Nindi was such a trusting little fellow. She didn't want to hurt his feelings by telling him what she really thought of the VIBs. Nindi wouldn't believe her anyway; he was just going to have to learn the hard way.

The following morning Yutta told Nindi that his first task was an important test of strength: he had to fly backwards and upside down for a distance of ten kilometres.

When Tilla looked up later that morning and saw Nindi upside down and flying backwards, with his eyeballs practically hanging out of his head, she couldn't help laughing.

'When will he learn?' she said to herself. 'If he doesn't give up soon he'll be dizzy for days.'

That night, as Nindi rested on the ground beside

her, Tilla said, 'You know, a bird can be important without belonging to a club'.

'But if you don't belong to a club no one knows you're important', Nindi replied as he closed his eyes.

'Of course you're important. I know you're important, that's all that matters.'

'But I don't feel important, and I won't feel important until I'm a VIB', Nindi said. Tilla sighed as Nindi added, 'By the way, Tilla, which way up am I now?'

Tilla gently pressed Nindi's beak into the ground and said 'Guess!'

The next day Nindi had to collect two hundred worms and hand-feed them to the VIBs. After that he had to make six large nests high up in the branches of a tall gum tree and fill each nest with four hundred berries exactly the same size. Finally, he had to duck-dive into a freezing cold pool until all the weeds had been picked from the bottom.

'Aaachoo!' he sneezed that night.

'Serves you right', said Tilla. 'You're not a water bird. I think you should give up this whole thing before you hurt yourself. They're never going to let you join!'

'N...n...naachooo! No! I'm nearly there. I might be a VIB tomorrow!'

'Or a VSB!'

'What's that?'

'Very Sick Bird!'

Tilla decided to follow Nindi the next day. She

wanted to keep an eye on her friend. She was worried things were getting serious.

Nindi still had the sniffles, but he cheered up considerably when Yutta said warmly, 'Today is a special day because we have a Very Important Task for a Very Important Bird!'

'That's me!' cried Nindi eagerly.

'Good!' Yutta praised the little bird. 'Now, follow me, but keep very quiet. Don't even sneeze!'

Nindi clamped his beak shut and, hardly breathing, followed Yutta and all the other VIBs to a clearing in the bush. Here Yutta pointed out a strange contraption made from paperbark and heavy twigs. One side was slightly propped up, giving a glimpse underneath of what appeared to be some very tasty food.

'Your mission, should you choose to accept it', said Yutta pompously, 'is to fly into that shelter and sample that food'.

'And then I'll be a VIB!'

Yutta just smiled sneakily.

What he hadn't told Nindi was that none of the VIBs could decide whether this contraption was a trap or not. They were all anxious to gobble up the delicious-looking seeds, but none of them wanted to risk being caught. Poor Nindi! He had no idea the VIBs were using him as a decoy.

Nindi was so excited he did a loop-the-loop before swooping down and squeezing under the shelter. The seeds were delicious. As he pecked away he called out to the VIBs, who were waiting nearby, 'Come on in, these seeds are great!'

'It must be safe after all', Yutta whispered to the others. 'If it wasn't, Nindi would be trapped by now. We'd better get in there fast, or he'll have all that wonderful food to himself!'

There was a loud flurry of wings, and within seconds all the VIBs were under the shelter, pecking and fighting with one another to get to the largest seeds.

In one swift movement the shelter closed over them and they were caught.

'It was a trap after all!' they shrieked in horror. 'It's all your fault, Nindi! It should have collapsed when you flew in, not us!'

Nindi backed into a dark corner and hid. It began to dawn on him how silly he'd been. And to think he might lose his life just because he wanted to be a VIB!

Suddenly, there was a scuffling noise outside. Everyone went very quiet.

'Are there any VIBs in there?' a familiar voice enquired.

'Of course there are!' screeched the VIBs. 'Get us out!'

'Are there any small birds in there who know who their real friends are?' asked Tilla, ignoring their cries for help.

Quietly, from a dark corner, a small voice said, 'I do'.

Tilla smiled to herself and lifted up the corner where the voice came from. Nindi squeezed out gratefully.

'What about us?' the others squawked in rage.

'Oh, you're all VIBs', said Tilla. 'You shouldn't need the help of an ordinary bird like me!'

Tilla and Nindi flew off, leaving the others to fight angrily among themselves.

'I've learnt my lesson', said Nindi mournfully.

'Yes, I believe you have', chuckled Tilla.

'The only thing is', added Nindi, 'I feel awful leaving the others there for the hunters. It just seems wrong, somehow.'

'I wouldn't worry about it', said Tilla confidently. 'It'll do them good to have a sleepless night!'

'But what about the hunters, won't they be back?'

'No doubt about it! The hunters who set that trap will be back, but not until late tomorrow. And before then those birds will be let out by a VCB.'

'A VCB?' queried Nindi in awe.

'A Very Clever Bird!' Tilla smiled smugly as she pointed to herself.

Nindi's eyes lit up with pleasure as he cried, 'Oh, Tilla, can I be a VCB too? Can I join your club, can I?'

Tilla roared with laughter and zoomed off, with Nindi following her calling, 'I was born clever you know, Tilla! Some birds are born beautiful, or even important, but me, I was born clever . . .'

# Gammin and brush

In the heavens long ago there lived a naughty child spirit called Gammin, who loved to tease and play tricks on others. He became such a nuisance, the Good Spirit decided it might help if Gammin had a friend to prevent him getting into mischief. So the Good Spirit created a being called Brush, who was strong enough to keep Gammin in line.

However, as you know, things don't always work out the way you think they will. Brush was certainly strong – but he was just as mischievous as Gammin!

The pair were soon inseparable. They spent their time zapping about the universe inventing surprises and playing tricks on everyone they met.

At first the Good Spirit was very tolerant. Whenever someone complained about Gammin and Brush's latest escapade he would say, 'Oh they're only young, they'll grow out of it'.

But time passed, and passed, and passed, and instead of growing more sensible the two friends grew sillier and sillier. One of their favourite hobbies became painting – they loved flicking great globs of colour at all the older spirits. The older spirits hated it because it made them visible. And this made it particularly difficult for them to eavesdrop on the Good Spirit's conversations without being noticed.

Things came to a head one morning when the Good Spirit woke up and discovered they'd painted rings around his new planet, Saturn.

'So!' he boomed when he finally found Brush and Gammin, 'you decided to improve on my handiwork, did you?'

Gammin chuckled sheepishly while Brush said outright, 'It looks better'.

'Well I don't think it looks better', growled the Good Spirit. 'I had plans for that planet. Why, oh why, do you do these things?'

'How would we know?' said Gammin. 'You made us, you tell us.'

'Yes', agreed Brush. 'Why do we do these things?'

The Good Spirit muttered under his breath and looked a trifle uncomfortable. 'Well', he murmured, 'when you're making things, combining one element with another, and so on, you're not always sure what the outcome will be'.

'You mean', said Brush, 'you never expected us to turn out the way we did?'

'Well . . . yes . . . I suppose you could put it like that.'

'But that explains everything, don't you see?' said Gammin. 'We were a surprise to you, so making surprises is in our nature. We just can't help ourselves!'

'Your natures are not irreversible', said the Good Spirit. 'All living matter has the potential to change. Nothing is fixed.'

'Hmph!' said Gammin in a superior voice. 'Brush might be living matter, but I'm not. I'm spirit like you!'

'Oh no you're not!' protested the Good Spirit. 'I conduct myself with dignity. I don't go flitting around the universe being a trickster.'

'You're spirit and I'm spirit', insisted Gammin. 'But Brush and Saturn aren't because they can't pass through things the way we can.'

'Look', interrupted the Good Spirit crossly, 'it really doesn't matter!'

'Exactly!' laughed Gammin. 'It doesn't matter because we're not matter, we're spirit.'

Gammin was so pleased with his cleverness that he began to do cartwheels all over the place.

Brush thought it looked like fun so he did the same. The Good Spirit sighed a long, deep, exasperated sigh and waited for them to stop.

'You must both understand', he said firmly when they'd exhausted themselves, 'that you cannot continue to do whatever you feel like doing. There has to be some order in the universe. If you both keep on the way you are, then where will we be?'

'Out of order!' they squealed and began cartwheeling again.

The Good Spirit laughed. But then he said, 'Gammin and Brush, you are delightful in small doses, but until you both learn to behave more responsibly you are limited to one surprise per heavenly cycle'.

Then he opened his mouth and with one quick puff blew them into outer space.

Gammin blinked hard as he floated softly in the cool blackness of deep space. Even though he opened his eyes as wide as he could, he could see no sign of light anywhere.

'What a hole', he muttered crossly to himself.

'Hole, hole, hole', the empty blackness echoed.

Gammin groaned and so did the blackness.

'Hey, this is fun!' he giggled.

'Fun, fun, fun', it echoed.

The word fun made Brush sit up and take notice. Soon he was calling out too. For half a cycle the two friends entertained themselves by teasing the blackness.

Gammin spent ages saying things like, 'Gammin's smart', 'Gammin's wise', 'Gammin's lovely'. He laughed with glee as the words smart, wise and lovely echoed around him. Brush just kept calling out, 'Fun, fun, fun'. That was all he was interested in.

But after the first half of the cycle in deep space they began to get bored with their new game. They agreed that if they were only allowed one surprise a cycle it would have to be a truly spectacular one. They began hunting throughout space for other beings to trick, tease or bewilder. They were terribly disappointed when they found they were quite alone.

'Let's head closer to home', suggested Gammin after a while. 'We're not going to find anything out here.'

They spun their way back as quickly as they could. The darkness surrounding them gradually grew lighter and lighter until up ahead they saw a huge asteroid.

'What a beauty!' cried Gammin in awe.

'It's bigger than Saturn! Let's paint it. We've never painted anything that big before', said Brush. 'What a challenge!'

'What a spectacular surprise it will be', giggled Gammin. 'Shall we do it in spots or stripes?'

'Neither', said Brush. 'I'm bored with them both.'

'What about circles or rings then?'

'No, we just did rings around Saturn, remember?'

'Then let's do something really different', cried Gammin. 'Let's paint it all one colour.'

'What a radical idea!' laughed Brush.

And soon they were sploshing bright red paint all over the enormous asteroid.

The asteroid was so huge that it took them the rest of their first cycle and nearly all of the second to complete.

Gammin and Brush lay back and admired their handiwork. It was their best painting ever. They congratulated themselves over and over. However, when it dawned on them that their second cycle was nearly over, they panicked. There was no way they wanted to miss out on their second cycle surprise.

'There's not enough time to hunt for something else to paint', moaned Brush. 'All that's out here is this asteroid and us!'

'That's it, Brush!' cried Gammin excitedly. 'Let's give the asteroid to the Good Spirit as a present. He'll love the colour.'

'You mean . . . move it out of its orbit . . . right up to him?' asked an incredulous Brush.

'That's just what I mean', said Gammin. 'It'll be the most surprising thing we've ever done!'

They became so caught up in the idea of giving the Good Spirit an enormous red ball that they conveniently forgot one of the cardinal rules of the universe. Make no surprise moves!

Brush had to use every bit of his power to budge the asteroid. Gammin helped by rocking it back and forth.

'Whoopee!' they yelled, as with a thunk and a clunk the Good Spirit's present finally jolted out of its usual orbit and began to roll forward.

At first the two friends easily kept pace with it, but it wasn't long before the asteroid began to go faster and faster, gathering speed with every roll, as it hurtled towards the Good Spirit's domain.

'Uh oh!' said Gammin.

Up ahead he saw Saturn, the ringed planet, right in the pathway of the speeding ball. Gammin and Brush gulped and closed their eyes. There was nothing they could do except hope. They both sighed with relief when the asteroid whizzed past, missing Saturn's rings by a hair's breadth.

'Thank heaven that's over', cried Gammin. 'I thought...', but he was interrupted by a terror-stricken scream from Brush. Gammin scanned the air in front of him and saw that the Good Spirit was holding one of his cosmic meetings directly in the pathway of the uncontrollable red asteroid.

Panting hard, Gammin and Brush sped as fast as they could, trying to catch up with their present, but it was no use. There was nothing to do but close their eyes to avoid seeing the terrible collision.

BANG! The explosion was gigantic, reverberating right throughout space. When the vibrations lessened, Gammin and Brush timidly opened their eyes. To their absolute amazement they saw that all there was left of the asteriod was a small red core, which had gone into orbit between Earth and Jupiter, and a lot of fine red powder was slowly drifting towards Earth.

The pair quickly looked for somewhere to hide. They knew that, if they were seen, everyone would automatically blame them. They hid behind a tiny, green-spotted asteroid and hoped that no one would notice their presence.

'Gammin . . . Brush . . .', a voice softly called. 'I want you both to come out . . . now!'

Nervously, they peered around the side of the tiny, green-spotted asteroid, only to see a very, very red Good Spirit bearing down on them.

He's gone red with rage, thought Gammin. But when he looked again he realised the Good Spirit was covered in a thick layer of fine red dust from the explosion.

'It . . . it . . . was meant to be a surprise', stuttered Gammin.

The Good Spirit raised his dusty eyebrows in disbelief.

'A good one', said Brush.

'Oh, it was a good one, all right', murmured the Good Spirit sarcastically. 'A big one too.'

'Very big', they agreed.

'Very big', mimicked the Good Spirit. 'And very red.'

'Just like you!' they said without thinking.

The Good Spirit's chin began to wobble. Then his lips began to shake. Then his mouth turned up at the corners. Soon he was chuckling and Gammin and Brush timidly began to smile too. Just to be on the safe side though, they rushed forward and began tickling him all over to keep him in a happy mood. Soon the three of them were laughing and sneezing.

As the last of the fine red dust blew away, the Good Spirit sneezed a final sneeze. Then he blew his nose, breathed deeply and smiled a secret smile.

'Mars', he said smugly, pointing to the bright red space ball happily spinning between Earth and Jupiter.

'Mars?' the friends chorused in surprise.

The Good Spirit moved forward and pointed down towards the middle of a large continent on the planet Earth.

'The Red Centre of Australia', he said happily.

Gammin and Brush looked at him suspiciously. They had a sneaky feeling that he had expected them to do what they had done, all along.

'Then it's all right?' they asked nervously. 'It doesn't matter, it really doesn't matter?'

'Oh let's not start that "matter" business again!' wheezed the Good Spirit.

And soon the three of them were laughing as helplessly as ever.

# A strange friendship

**M**arlu and Willie were the best of friends. Marlu was a rather large kangaroo who loved the open plains. He was rough and tough and one hundred per cent pure muscle. His nickname was 'Big Red' because he was one of the strongest and best fighters around. His friend, Willie, was a small, dark bird who insisted on wagging his tail just like a dingo. He wasn't much to look at but he was a good singer. He'd been nicknamed 'Willie Wagtail' by Billen the budgerigar, who was very jealous of Willie's beautiful voice.

I suppose you're wondering why two such different creatures would want to be friends? After all, red kangaroos are supposed to look down on tiny birds. Well, the answer is simple. They each had something the other admired.

Marlu loved music. When he listened to Willie singing he felt as if he was floating on air. He might be Big Red, the big, tough fighter, but he was also going to be Marlu, the amazing singer.

Willie, on the other hand, loved muscles. He desperately wanted his whole tiny, feathery body to be one great, big, hard muscle. Billen would think twice before picking on him then.

The two friends decided there was no reason why they shouldn't share their separate skills. Willie was very confident that he could teach Marlu the singing tricks his mother had taught him when he was very young. And Marlu knew plenty of exercises that he was positive would make Willie strong. They both believed that practice makes perfect. And while Willie was a bit weak to start off with, and Marlu was unable to sing in tune, they were sure that in no time at all they'd be entirely different creatures.

Every week they met to practise exercising and singing. And, just between you and me, I don't know which was funnier: Willie lying on his back lifting stones up and down with his tiny feet, or Marlu with his mouth wide open, groaning and gargling.

They'd been practising for weeks when one day Billen flew past and stopped to look. He'd been attracted by the sound of someone in pain. He didn't realise, until he took a good look, that it was actually Marlu trying to sing.

Pathetic, he thought nastily as he covered his head with his wing to drown out the sound. That kangaroo must have muscles in his head. He decided to fly off and find something else to do. However, just as he was about to leave, he spotted his old enemy, Willie Wagtail, lying on the ground.

'Oh good, he's dead!' twittered Billen meanly. 'Marlu must have stood on him.' But to his disappointment he saw Willie's tired little legs grasp a small pebble and begin pumping. This really had Billen puzzled. What on earth was Willie doing?

Marlu answered Billen's question for him when he stopped trying to sing and said, 'That's good, Willie, old pal. Keep it up. In no time at all you'll be strong enough to do whatever you like with Billen!'

'Hmph!' muttered Billen crossly to himself as he flew off. 'So that's what it's all about. Thinks he's going to beat me up does he? Well, that horrible, nasty little songbird has got another think coming! I'll soon put a stop to his little plan. Willie Wagtail's not going to outsmart me. I should be able to think of something. I'm very good at being sneaky!'

In fact, sneakiness was one of Billen's outstanding qualities and by the following morning he'd thought of a wonderfully underhand plan. He got up early, just before sunrise, and flew directly to the feeding ground of Marlu's herd of kangaroos.

He went straight up to Gulub, the leader, and said sweetly, 'How's the choir going?'

Gulub ignored him and went on chewing grass.

Billen chirped louder. 'I said, how's the choir going?'

Gulub stopped chewing and looked at him out of the corner of his eye. You snivelling little twit, he thought.

Never one to miss an opportunity, Billen said at the top of his voice, 'Do you sing in the kangaroo choir too, Gulub?'

The great kangaroo reared back on his strong tail and snorted hard at Billen, who tumbled over several times in the air.

But the little bird was determined not to be put off. He smoothed down his ruffled feathers as best he could and came back with, 'It's true! You can snort as much as you like, but that won't change anything. You ask Marlu, he's a musical kangaroo. If you're nice to him he might even sing you to sleep at night'.

'Tired of life are you, Billen?' asked Gulub angrily. 'Well, say your prayers because if you don't put a lid on it, I'm going to send you to heaven!'

Faced with Gulub's clenched fist, Billen squawked in fright, 'It's true, it's true! All of it. His best friend is Willie Wagtail!'

Gulub drew back his paw. Either Billen deserved all he got, or he was telling the truth.

'Willie Wagtail?' asked Gulub. 'The bird who seems to think he's a dog?'

'Y . . . yes, that's him', stuttered Billen. 'And an evil, more horrid little bird you couldn't hope to meet!'

Just then Marlu bounded up. When he heard Billen twitter uncontrollably and saw Gulub looking at him suspiciously, he began to feel rather uncomfortable.

'Big Red', said Gulub firmly, 'what's all this nonsense about a kangaroo choir? Please tell me this gossip isn't true and that you haven't been singing with silly Willie?' Gulub had every confidence in Marlu. He had even singled him out to be the new leader after he himself became too old.

Marlu's colour changed to a deep, blushing red. 'It's not exactly a choir', he replied. 'It's more like . . . singing lessons. He's teaching me to sing and I'm teaching him how to exercise . . .' Marlu's voice trailed away pitifully as Gulub snorted, 'Big and thick, that's what you are! All brawn and no brain! We're fighting kangaroos, not big, furry songsters. I suppose you'll be perching in a tree next!'

Marlu felt very embarrassed in front of his leader. How could I have been so stupid, he thought. Kangaroos are fighters not singers. He cringed with shame when he remembered his secret ambition to be a dancer as well. Thank heavens Billen hadn't seen him pointing his toes.

'We'll be the laughing stock of the bush if this ever gets out!' shouted Gulub. Suddenly he remembered Billen. He swung towards him, but Billen was already flying away squawking, 'Kangaroo choir for hire, kangaroo choir for hire!'

Willie was completely unaware of what had happened, so when he saw Marlu a day later he called out as he normally did, 'How's your singing going, old pal?'

Marlu blushed fiercely and grunted through his teeth, 'Be quiet!'

Willie didn't hear him properly so he fluttered down and said, 'You're not sick are you, Marlu? It'd be terrible if your teeth were stuck together and you couldn't practise your singing. How are your legs feeling? What about a bit of a dance?'

Marlu grabbed Willie in his fist and clamped one claw over his beak. 'Listen, you stupid bird', he said as nastily as he could. 'Creatures like us aren't meant to be friends. Now why don't you go find a dingo to play with?'

Willie was stunned. What had happened to his old mate?

'B . . . b . . . but', he whispered, still unable to believe that Marlu had changed, 'I want you to look at my tail. I think those exercises you showed me have made it stronger'. Marlu's grip had loosened, so Willie flew up and wagged his tail in the kangaroo's face.

'Will you never learn?' shouted Marlu in anger. 'I don't want to be friends any more. And if you don't leave me alone, you won't have a tail to wag!' Marlu bared his big, kangaroo teeth.

Willie sobbed and whimpered, 'I'm going, I'm going'. And, downcast, he flew away.

From then on Willie only saw Marlu from a distance. It made him very sad to see his old friend so unhappy. Marlu was picking fights with everyone to prove he was a fighter, not a sissy singer. Willie felt terribly sorry for him.

Just before sunset one evening, Willie was perched in a tree overlooking the kangaroos' favourite water-hole when he saw six men sneak up and hide in the thick bushes just below him. Being a curious bird, Willie fluttered a little closer. They were talking about kangaroo steaks, and when he saw their sharp spears he knew why. They were hunters waiting for their victims to come in to drink.

Willie's small heart pounded furiously. What could he do? He wasn't strong enough yet to take them all on.

Oh no, he thought in horror as he heard a THUMP! THUMP! THUMP! Gulub's bringing them in early!

Without a second thought for his own safety he flew from his tree directly towards the incoming roos. As he went he sang as loudly as he could. It was a warning song his mother had taught him and he desperately hoped Marlu would recognise it.

'There's that silly bird–dog again. This'll be his swan-song', muttered Gulub under his breath when he saw Willie coming. He still hadn't forgiven the small bird for shaming them. Gulub curled his right fist over as he bounded closer and closer. But suddenly Marlu understood what Willie was singing and shouted out, 'Hunters! Willie's warning us. There are hunters at the waterhole!' The kangaroos veered away just as the men rushed out and threw their cruel spears. Two roos were wounded, but they all managed to escape to safety.

The kangaroos didn't return to the water-hole until they were sure the hunters had gone. And when they did they searched in the darkness for one small bird. 'Willie', they called softly. 'Willie Wagtail . . .' There was no reply.

'They must have got him', said Marlu, who was on the verge of tears. 'He's probably lying in two halves on the ground somewhere.' They all felt terrible.

'I never thought I'd ask this, Big Red', said Gulub in a husky voice. 'But would you mind singing? If he is alive, that's the only thing he'll answer to.'

Marlu felt a little embarrassed as he threw his big kangaroo head back and let out a loud groaning sound that grew higher and higher in pitch until it ended in a final, drawn-out, tiny wail. The others covered their ears and tried not to smile. Kangaroos were definitely not singers.

They listened intently in the darkness for any sound of Willie, but there was none. All anyone could hear was the occasional chirrup of a cricket.

Two big, fat kangaroo tears rolled down Marlu's furry cheeks. He felt absolutely miserable. He'd lost his best friend in the whole world.

'What was that?' asked Gulub suddenly.

'What?' questioned Marlu.

'That faint sound. Listen, it's so beautiful.'

The faint, joyful warble grew louder and louder until, magically, Willie flew in out of the darkness and landed somewhat unsteadily on Marlu's shoulder. Two of his larger tail feathers were missing.

'WILLIE!' they all cried in joy.

'Just as well my tail is pure muscle', he said cheekily. 'Otherwise I might have lost the lot!'

From then on all the kangaroos enjoyed Willie's singing. None of them had ever really listened to him before and they had to admit that they rather liked it. Marlu continued to love music but gave up singing. And Willie never bothered exercising any more because with friends like the red kangaroos he had no trouble at all keeping Billen in line.

# Gorban and the gilbingooras

**G**orban was a big, boastful red giant who lived in a mountain cave. His arms and legs were as thick as tree trunks, his fingers were as fat as melons and his stomach was as big as a hill. His favourite saying was 'Big is best', and he shouted this in a thunderous voice every night from his mountain top, causing the valley below to shake.

Tiny people called Gilbingooras lived in the valley. They could make themselves invisible whenever they liked, which was probably the only reason they were still alive. They tormented other creatures so often with their silly tricks that they were rarely out of danger or trouble, and Gorban was one of their favourite targets.

Every morning they waited for him to come down to drink at his favourite water-hole. 'He's coming, he's coming. Ssh, ssh', they'd warn each other as they hid in the bushes with their spears ready. As soon as Gorban got down on his hands and knees to drink, they'd rush out with blood-curdling yells and poke their tiny spears into his huge backside, chanting, 'Spiky bum, spiky bum!'

Gorban was not amused. He'd often thought about shooting them into outer space with one short, sharp puff, but he'd never bothered. They were too small and silly for him to waste his breath on. Besides, their spears were less than pinpricks to him.

When the Gilbingooras weren't being naughty they were bored.

'I'm bored', said one of them one morning.

'Me too, me too!' the others chorused. They liked to copy one another.

'I know', the first one said. 'Let's change colour. I want to be pink!'

'Me too, me too!' the others agreed.

They collected pink, wild bush-berries, ground them into a fine paste, and plastered the stuff all over their brown bodies.

'I'm going to be pink for ever', said one excitedly.

'Pink for ever, pink for ever!' the others chanted.

'I like being pink and silly', giggled a Gilbingoora as a great dollop of pink syrup rolled down his forehead, clung to the tip of his nose and then, just as it was about to drop, landed with a squelch on a quickly outstretched pink tongue. 'Ooh yum', he said. 'I taste good.'

'Taste good, taste good!' the others chanted as they began to lick themselves all over. Gilbingooras were not fussy eaters.

They were so busy being silly that no one noticed a giant eagle flying overhead looking for food. Normally the eagle wouldn't have noticed the Gilbingooras because their little brown bodies blended in perfectly with the bush. But today when she looked down and saw what she thought were bright pink worms she dropped from the sky like a lightning bolt. She scooped them all up with her claws and soared back up into the heavens, not stopping until she'd reached her nest high on Gorban's mountain.

'We're going to be eaten, we're going to be eaten!' they all babbled as she dropped them onto her eggs and flew off in search of more food. They were so frightened they began punching and kicking one another until finally one of them moaned, 'I hurt'.

'Me too, me too!' the others responded.

They stopped fighting just as suddenly as they'd

started and decided to stand on one another's shoulders so the top one could see where they were.

'Eeek!' he screamed as he peered over the edge of the nest.

'Eek, eek, eek!' the others screeched when he told them they were on top of Gorban's mountain.

'What are we going to do?' someone asked.

'Nothing we can do', the others said. 'Nothing, nothing, nothing!' Even their magic men couldn't help because they had dropped their bags of pastes and potions as the eagle swept them up. The Gilbingooras all began fighting among themselves again.

Just then the sound of distant thunder rolled up the mountain. The Gilbingooras stopped pulling each other's hair out and listened in fear. There it was again, only louder and closer.

'It's Gorban', someone said. 'He must be coming up to his cave.'

Within minutes Gorban's big nose blocked out the sun and his two beady eyes peered into the nest.

'Soooo', he said as they all tried to hide under the eggs. 'Pink Gilbingooras!'

Gorban smiled smugly at their frightened faces. He always knew their silliness would be the end of them some day.

'The eagle thinks she has some nice, fat, juicy pink worms for her breakfast', he teased. 'But if

she eats you she'll probably choke to death!'
Gorban laughed. Then he reached in and began to
remove the eggs one by one, putting them in his
dillybag. Eggs were his favourite food and he was
planning to have these for his supper.

'Please help us', the Gilbingooras pleaded.
'Please, please, please!' But Gorban ignored them
and went on collecting the eggs.

'You have us to thank for these eggs', a very
brave Gilbingoora shouted.

'Thank for these eggs, thank for these eggs', the
others copied.

'Oh', said Gorban as he raised his hairy eyebrows. 'Why? Did you lay them?' He began to
chuckle at the thought.

'They'd have gone rotten if we hadn't sat on
them', someone said.

'Rotten, rotten, rotten!'

Gorban shook his head in disbelief. Did they
really think he'd fall for that one? He pulled out
the last egg and went to turn away.

'Don't leave us!' they all screeched in terror.
'You might need our help one day!'

Gorban found this idea amusing. 'Big is best',
he said. 'Small is stupid.'

The Gilbingooras flopped back in despair on
the floor of the nest. They were done for. Gorban
had been their only hope.

Gorban sighed and looked at them out of the
corner of his eye. He was cross because he was

beginning to feel sorry for them and he didn't really want to. They don't really deserve my help, he thought. It serves them right for making my backside feel like I'd sat on an echidna.

One of the silliest Gilbingooras suddenly sat up and bent over and began sucking his big toe, whimpering at the same time. Soon they were all doing it. It was pitiful.

'Oh all right', grunted Gorban reluctantly. 'I'll help you this time, but never again!' He held out his little finger and told them to climb onto it. One small, quick puff and they tumbled down the mountainside and landed in a slippery pink heap on top of a prickle bush.

'Ouch, yikes!' they complained as they untangled themselves. 'Old spiky bum did that on purpose!' They grumbled all the way home about the prickles, the eagle and how they now owed grumpy Gorban a favour.

It was about this time that the first humans arrived in the country of Gorban and the Gilbingooras. Now, humans had pretty strange ideas in those days. Apart from the wildlife, they thought they were the only beings in existence. Because they never doubted their own view of the world, they never saw the tiny Gilbingooras, even when they were visible, and they didn't believe in giants either. Every evening when Gorban shouted 'Big is best', the humans just thought it was thunder rumbling through the mountains. The Gilbingooras were very interested in the humans, but they could tell they were different from Gorban and themselves. They often talked about this at night.

'Yesterday', said a Gilbingoora one night, 'I jumped onto a human's nose and pulled faces at him. He didn't see me. He just sneezed and blew me off into the bush'.

'No manners, no manners!' the others responded.

'I bit one on the ankle the other day', said a second. 'He never gave me any attention at all. He just brushed me away like a fly.'

'Like a fly, like a fly!' they repeated.

'I'm not going to play with them any more', said another Gilbingoora, who was sick of the humans ignoring him.

'Don't play, don't play!' they all agreed.

And so the humans continued to remain completely unaware that Gorban or the Gilbingooras existed. They would have stayed like this for ever had they not begun to take notice of the large footprints that appeared around their favourite waterhole each morning. They became so troubled by these tracks that they were soon discussing what they should do about them.

'It must be a huge animal that eats everything it sees', one human suggested.

'It likes eggs too', said another as he pointed to the ground. 'Look at all these crushed shells. We won't be safe until we get rid of it'.

They all agreed. But how? Someone suggested poisoning the water-hole, but as they all drank from it this was declared a silly idea.

'Eggs are easy to find', said another as he held up a handful of shell. 'And the huge animal obviously likes them. We'll poison lots and lots of eggs! We'll inject them with snake venom to make sure they're really deadly. And then we'll hide them under the bushes near the water-hole.'

When Gorban next came down to drink, the smell of eggs was very strong. He licked his lips and sniffed and sniffed until he found them. There were eggs of every size, shape and colour hidden under some thick bushes. Gorban was delighted.

'Yum', he said as he began loading them into his dillybag. 'These eggs probably belong to the humans, but, as I'm sharing my country with them, they can share their eggs with me. Maybe they even put them here to say thank you.'

The humans were very pleased the following day when they saw that all the eggs had been taken.

'There really is a huge animal', they said to each other as they left. 'But, he'll be dead by now.'

As usual, the Gilbingooras waited with their little spears ready for Gorban when he came down to the water-hole to drink. They were bitterly disappointed when, after several days, he failed to arrive.

'Where is he? Where is he?' they asked. 'Where's spiky bum?' As they grew tired of waiting they began chanting crossly, 'Spoil-sport, spoil-sport!'

'I'm going to tell spiky bum what I think of him', said one of the Gilbingooras crossly. 'I'm going up the mountain!'

'Up the mountain, up the mountain!' they yelled angrily as they stormed off.

It took them more than a week to reach the top of the mountain.

'We're here, we're here!' they all shouted as they ran inside the enormous, dark cave that was Gorban's home.

Gorban was lying on his back in the middle of the floor and he was very still. Without stopping to wonder why this was so, the Gilbingooras began yelling, 'Spoil-sport, spoil-sport!' as they swarmed all over him, poking their little spears in wherever they could.

'Say something, say something!' they urged as their frenzied prodding finally died down.

There was silence. Gorban didn't move. One of the Gilbingoora magic men crawled up to his mouth and sat on the giant's top lip. Using the blunt end of his spear he pushed down the giant's bottom lip and sniffed deeply.

'Ooh, poo', he said. 'He smells like snake venom.'

Gorban's eyes flickered and he moaned slightly. Gilbingooras, he thought in disgust. Why couldn't they just let him die in peace?

'He's alive, he's alive!' they all shouted when they saw his eyelids quiver. A group of them rushed to his head and pulled one lid open by yanking on the eyelashes. They spoke encouragingly to the sick eyeball. 'Gilbingoora magic can fix poison', they said. Plonk! The lid slid shut, flinging one Gilbingoora down to the giant's foot.

'Do that again and we won't use our magic', said another crossly to the lid.

'No good, anyway', said the magic man. 'He's too big. Can't mix enough paste to cover him in one go.'

For once there was complete silence. The magic man was right. Gorban was just too big!

'Do him in bits!' someone suddenly shouted.

'Stupid, stupid!' another replied. 'What if some bits die while we're covering other bits?'

'Half a giant is better than no giant at all', said the magic man. 'Half a giant could be a lot of fun.'

'Start with the feet', one of them giggled. 'That way he can still come down to the water-hole and bend over.'

'No, no', objected others. 'Head and mouth first. Otherwise he won't be able to say "Big is best" and our valley will stop shaking.' They loved to roll around on the trembling earth just before they went to sleep.

While they all argued Gorban was slowly dying. Fortunately for him, however, there was finally a united cry of 'In the middle!', and they set to work.

To their credit they worked very, very hard gathering all the ingredients for the magic paste and mixing them together over a fire. By the following morning Gorban's stomach had changed from a sickening green to its usual red earth colour.

'It's hungry', said the magic man as he prodded the giant's stomach and made it gurgle. 'We'd better feed him some of those eggs we collected.'

They all rushed up to his lips and quickly covered them with magic paste. 'Can't swallow, can't swallow!' they all shouted in horror when they realised the throat was nearly dead.

With great haste they pasted a pathway all the way down Gorban's throat to his stomach. Then one by one they shoved fresh, healthy eggs into his mouth.

'Hoo, this is fun', they giggled as someone accidentally shoved an egg up Gorban's nose.

By the following morning Gorban was sitting up, red all over except for his legs, which were still a deathly green colour. For the first time in days he spoke. 'What's in that paste?' he asked curiously.

'Worm guts, ant brains, hairy mosquito legs, slime and festering mud', they replied. It was the last question Gorban asked for a while.

'Feel a bit dead in the legs?' they asked cheekily as they continued to paste.

'Dead legs, dead legs', they all giggled.

Gorban groaned. Their jokes were so weak.

'Be nice to us', they warned him. 'Otherwise we'll leave you like this and you'll have to roll everywhere.' This ridiculous idea made them all stop and think. It'd be fun to have a rolling giant. They could use him to flatten all sorts of things.

'You promised to help all of me', Gorban reminded them quickly. 'Not just half.'

By the next day Gorban was his old self.

'Big is still best', he told them. 'But for Gilbingooras small is tall.'

'Small is tall, small is tall!' they sang in glee.

Gorban smiled. He knew they'd love a saying that made no sense.

That evening Gorban and the Gilbingooras stood in front of the cave. While he bellowed 'Big is best', they screamed 'Small is tall'. They all shouted so long and loudly that a thundering storm blew up. It ripped through the valley below, knocking down trees and flinging the humans around like twigs. By the time the giant and his friends had finished yelling all the humans were running away from the country of Gorban and the Gilbingooras as fast as their legs would carry them!

# The cocky who loved gossip

Cocky was a great talker. He had an opinion on everything, and he wasn't backward in telling others what someone had said about them. He loved secrets but he never kept them. And he was a terrible eavesdropper. In fact, Cocky was what's commonly known as a gossip.

Gossips are bad listeners because they only hear what they want to hear. They like juicy titbits of information: tender, flavoursome morsels they can exaggerate into a feast; short, sharp sentences about others, not long, boring paragraphs about the weather or cooking recipes. Moreover, gossips are always innocent. After all, they're only passing on what they've heard. They believe very strongly in freedom of information, so they make sure the 'right' people hear what they think they should hear.

One warm spring morning, as he was flying through the bush looking for a conversation he could get his beak into, Cocky spotted a small group of mothers talking eagerly.

'They look as though they're having a full-blown mothers' meeting', Cocky said to himself. 'I'd better listen. I'm bound to hear something good.' He hid himself among the thick, yellow flowers of a nearby wattle tree and waited. He was fairly high up and the wind was blowing, but Cocky was able to catch snippets of the conversation going on below. He could tell that Kangaroo, Pelican, Wombat and Dingo were all talking excitedly.

'...big hairy feet...biggest I've ever seen...' Kangaroo's voice floated up.

'...mouth the size of a cave...' Sounded like Pelican talking, Cocky thought.

'...as fat as a hill...', Wombat's voice wafted up.

'...the longest, bushiest tail I've ever seen...'

Who's Dingo accusing of having the bushiest tail, Cocky wondered, his head buzzing. What a minefield of information he'd stumbled on! But what did it all mean? And, more importantly, who were all these creatures they were talking about? He flew off to puzzle over what he'd heard.

'Big, hairy feet', he repeated to himself as he glided with the wind. 'Big, hairy feet. Who could Kangaroo have been talking about?'

Just then Cocky looked down and saw Emu picking up seeds from the ground with his pointy beak. Of course, thought Cocky. It was Emu! Kangaroo must be very jealous of him.

Cocky swooped down and squawked, 'Huge, hairy feet, huge, hairy feet. Feet as hairy and spiky as spinifex balls, that's what you've got!'

Emu glared at him and went on pecking.

But Cocky was determined to get his attention, so he squawked even louder, 'Feet as hairy as a possum's backside!'

That was too much for Emu. He raised one large foot over the small bird, causing Cocky to screech, 'Not me, not me. Oh no, it wasn't me! Kangaroo said it!'

Emu snorted in disgust and rested his foot back on the ground. He was deeply insulted. His smooth, large feet were his pride and joy. Fancy Kangaroo being that nasty, thought Emu. Then he turned to Cocky and said, 'I'll make sure Kangaroo gets what's coming to her, don't you worry!'

'Too right!' whistled Cocky. And he flew off to puzzle over the next saying.

'Mouth as big as a cave', he muttered over and over. Ooh, that was a hard one. But then he saw Python stretched out on a flat rock, sunning herself.

'Ho, ho, ho', said Cocky. 'So that's who Pelican doesn't like!' He fluttered down, careful not to get too close because Python was looking rather hungry.

'Mouth as big as a giant cave', he said loudly. 'Big mouth, big mouth!'

Python hissed and reared up. She was very sensitive about her mouth.

'Not me, not me!' screeched Cocky, who suddenly realised that Python was a little longer than he'd thought. 'I'm only telling you what Pelican said!'

'Sssssooooo', spat Python. 'That's what she thinks, is it? I'll teach her a lesson that'll take her breath away.'

Cocky chose that moment to disappear. He was a bit worried Python might like to take his breath away too.

'What a day', he sighed as he swooped up and down. 'I love chatting!' Then he began to think about Wombat's comment, 'Fat as a hill, fat as a hill!' Over and over he sang his little refrain, but in the end he had to admit that he really didn't know to whom it referred. A faint, scratching sound drifted up to him. When he looked down he saw Brush Turkey frantically digging for worms.

Yippee, thought Cocky. There's my answer. Wombat must hate Turkey because she's really very slim under those bushy feathers.

Cocky dropped down and walked right up to Turkey.

'Morning', he said cheerfully.

'Morning', said Turkey, who went on scratching. She was far too hungry to talk.

'Got some news', said Cocky enticingly.

'Go away', replied Turkey. 'Can't you see I'm hunting!'

'Yes', replied Cocky. 'Food is all you think about. Food, food, food! You're as fat as . . . as . . . a . . . bloated fish!'

Turkey's head shot bolt upright. Her eyes sparkled angrily as she said, 'My beak is also very sharp!' She took one large step towards Cocky but he yelled, 'Not me, not me. Oh no, it wasn't me! Wombat said it. She's telling everyone!'

'I had no idea that lump of lard was so jealous of my good figure', Turkey said hotly. 'I'll soon whittle her down to size!'

Cocky nodded in agreement and flew off. Turkey was quite right, he thought. People should get their just desserts!

As he flew on, the words 'long, bushy tail' kept flitting through his brain. Before long he found he was humming, 'Long, bushy tail. Long, bushy tail', over and over. He hummed for several hours but absolutely no inspiration came to him. Cocky hated to be beaten when it came to this kind of puzzle. His throat was sore and dry, and his brain tired from thinking, so he decided to drop down and have a long, cool drink from the river. Perhaps the water would refresh him.

As he was guzzling thirstily away, old Water Rat popped his head up and said, 'Been a warm day, eh, Cocky?'

'Yep', said Cocky, whose beak was still full. He gulped down the last of his drink and turned to look at Rat, who was busy cleaning his whiskers.

Aah haa! he thought when he spied Rat's tail. Dingo must hate Rat because with the help of his tail Rat can swim faster than she can!

'Long and bushy! As long as . . . as a snake, and as bushy as . . . as a bottlebrush!' squawked Cocky hoarsely.

'What is?' asked Rat.

'Your tail!'

Rat shoved his big front teeth forward and crouched down ready to spring.

'Not me!' whistled Cocky urgently. 'It's never me! Dingo said it. I just thought you should know.'

'My tail is sleek and slim', said Rat proudly. 'Long enough to help me swim and thin enough to keep me out of trouble.' Then with a splash he disappeared back under the water. As he dived deeper and deeper, he felt hurt and surprised that Dingo could be such a beast. It's time someone taught her a lesson, Rat decided.

Cocky flew off, feeling tired but terribly elated. What a day! He'd solved all the puzzles. All he needed now was a quiet place to rest for the night.

He drifted off to sleep in the branches of his favourite gum tree, hoping that tomorrow would be as exciting.

It so happened that the following morning the four mothers, Kangaroo, Pelican, Wombat and Dingo, were walking through the bush, chattering once again.

'Oh hello', called Kangaroo when she saw Emu, Python, Turkey and Water Rat up ahead. 'Lovely morning.'

'Lovely morning, indeed!' snorted Emu as he thumped the ground with one smooth foot.

Python reared up and hissed angrily when she saw Pelican. Turkey screeched loudly when she noticed Wombat. And Rat sharpened his teeth when he saw Dingo.

Within seconds there were feathers, fur and insults flying everywhere. There was screaming and shouting, squeezing and pecking, pulling and biting. Emu trod crossly on Kangaroo's big feet. Python wound her long, thick body tightly around Pelican and squeezed so hard poor Pelican began to turn blue. Turkey grasped Wombat with her feet and pecked Wombat's plump round body with her beak. And Rat sank his big front teeth into Dingo's tail and chewed off large chunks of hair. The fight only ended when they were all too wounded and exhausted to keep going.

'That'll teach you to say my beautiful big feet

are hairy', spat Emu as he gave Kangaroo one last prod.

'But I didn't', protested Kangaroo. 'I wouldn't . . .'

'And assss for you, Pelican', hissed Python. 'You know my mouth is only large when I eat.'

'I know', gasped Pelican, who was just getting her breath back. 'I haven't . . . said . . . a word . . . about your mouth!'

'I have a lovely figure', boasted Turkey, and she held herself erect so as to appear slimmer. 'You're the one that's fat, Wombat!'

Wombat moaned and licked her bleeding paw.

'My tail is sleek and slim', said Rat proudly as he held it up, 'not bushy like yours, Dingo!'

'I don't know what any of you are talking about', Dingo whined.

'None of us know what you're talking about', sighed Kangaroo. 'Who ever told you such things?'

'Cocky', they chorused.

'Cocky?' the others repeated in disbelief.

There was silence. They all remembered that Cocky had caused trouble before. Emu, Python, Turkey and Rat all began to look a little sheepish. They had all been far too keen to believe the worst.

The explanation suddenly dawned on Kangaroo. 'I know what happened!' she said. 'Yesterday we were all talking about our babies, remember? I'm sure I saw Cocky sitting in the wattle tree just near us. He must have eavesdropped and taken everything we said the wrong way!' Kangaroo turned to Emu and said crossly, 'I was talking about my son's feet, not yours. It's good for a kangaroo to have big, hairy feet!'

'And my child has a huge mouth to catch fish with, thank goodness!' cried Pelican.

'And', growled Wombat, 'my little girl is as fat as a hill and proud of it!'

'And my boy has the longest, bushiest tail!' moaned Dingo last as she looked sadly at her mangled tail.

Just then, Cocky flew in. He'd had a wonderful night's sleep, but the day had been going badly. He'd been flying around for ages and hadn't heard one interesting thing.

'Any news?' he asked innocently. When he saw all their cuts and bruises he said excitedly, 'Ooh, what's been happening here?'

'ARGH!' they all screamed as they rushed madly at him. Cocky was so shocked that they would attack an innocent bird that he forgot all about flying. Instead, he turned and ran squawking into the bush shouting, 'Not me! Not me! Oh no, it's never, ever me!'

You'll be pleased to know that Cocky did get his just desserts that day. Gossips always do in the end. So the next time you overhear something you shouldn't, perhaps you'd better think twice before you believe it.

# Shontu the greedy
# crocodile

**W**hen Shontu the crocodile finally hatched from his egg, his mother thought he was the sweetest of all her little crocs hatched that day. But she soon changed her mind when he sank his sharp little teeth into her tail and began chewing. Imagine being so greedy that you'd take a bite out of your own mother!

Much to his family's horror, Shontu became even worse as he grew older. He lost all his old playmates because he kept trying to eat them, and it was very hard for him to make new friends because no one trusted him. Whenever he tried to hug or kiss other crocodiles his own age they screamed and ran away.

Shontu had absolutely no manners at all. He never said 'Excuse me' when he burped or farted, and he loved popping rotten, smelly bits of mouldy food into his mouth to suck on. It was no wonder the other little crocodiles chanted a nasty rhyme when they saw him:

> Suck your dirty teeth,
> Suck your dirty teeth,
> Slobber and slurp, dribble and burp,
> Suck your dirty teeth!

However, Shontu soon gave up this foul sucking habit in favour of something better – a full stomach. But, as everyone knows, food needs chewing, and chewing takes time. To save time Shontu began swallowing his food whole, snapping up anything that moved.

Of course, the victim, whether swallowed whole or chewed, found the end equally gruesome. After all there's not much to choose between being mashed to a bloody pulp of flesh and bone or drowned in digestive juices that smell like stale vomit.

At first swallowing his food whole made poor Shontu burp and fart non-stop. However, the more food he swallowed whole, the more his body grew used to it. Eventually he managed to keep the buildup of putrid air down in his stomach, letting it out only at night in great big, foul belches.

Now, the place where Shontu lived was the country of the Noongal family. They were a very large family with lots of grannies and grandpas, mothers and fathers, brothers and sisters, uncles and aunts, cousins, grandchildren and dogs. One of the grannies was called Granny Wongon and she had been fighting with Shontu since the day he was born.

When he was very young, Shontu had bitten off most of the tail of her pet dingo. Granny Wongon had tried to catch the crocodile to teach him a lesson but he was too cunning even then.

Over the years Granny Wongon complained about Shontu to her family but no one would listen. She was worried that if something wasn't done he'd grow into a monster. Everyone told her to mind her own business and let Shontu's parents sort him out.

But a time eventually came when Shontu's parents disappeared in very mysterious circumstances.

Left to his own devices Shontu grew bigger and bigger until he was so enormous he was a danger to every living thing. He was an exceptional hunter and one of his cherished dreams was to swallow Granny Wongon and her whole extended family. It was just as well they had a warning system. Dingo had had a sixth sense about the crocodile ever since he'd lost most of his tail. I suppose these days we might call it 'dingo radar', because whenever Shontu was near, the stubby left-over bit of tail, and every hair on it, would stand straight up in alarm.

Every day Shontu searched for the Noongal family and every day he caught all the food he could ever want, except them. By evening, he would be terribly bad tempered and would fling himself on the ground in frustration, rolling over and over until he'd flattened everything in sight. Then he'd stalk back angrily to the silence of the river, leaving behind him a path of terrible destruction.

'We've got to do something about that monster', Granny Wongon complained urgently to her family one night. 'If he keeps on the way he's going we won't have anything left to eat.'

No one replied. They just continued to stare into the mesmerising flames of the fire. She was right, of course, but what could they do? When he was young they had had a chance but it was too late now. The crocodile was huge and his hide was so tough that even their sharpest spears would bounce off it.

'Dingo always warns us', Ginari, one of her grandsons, finally said trying to placate her.

'But Dingo's getting old', she replied as she patted the dog affectionately. 'What will we do when he dies?'

'We don't know!' said her sister impatiently. It was all too much for her. 'We'll think about it after Dingo is gone!'

Unfortunately, Dingo went the next day. He'd been wandering absent-mindedly through the bush, not paying enough attention to his tail, when he walked straight into the crocodile's open mouth and silently disappeared. All that remained were a few shocked brown hairs standing straight up among the dribble on the ground.

Granny Wongon was terribly upset. Dingo was her best friend. She wailed and wailed and all her sisters wailed with her. 'We'll get you another pup', they cried. 'One that looks just like Dingo.'

'I don't want another pup', she sobbed. 'I just want Dingo. We must rescue him!'

'NO!' they all cried in horror. 'That's a stupid idea!'

Granny Wongon glared at them.

'He'll be dead by now anyway, Granny', said Ginari, who had come over to sit with her for a while.

'Not my Dingo', she replied. 'He's a strong fella. He could swim in Shontu's stomach for hours and not get tired. There'd be plenty of smelly air in there to keep him going.'

'Even so', said one of the men, 'none of us is silly enough to risk his life rescuing a dog that might die soon anyway. Besides, he's no good to us now – his tail's probably not working any more. How else would he have got caught?'

'And what if it were me in there?' Granny Wongon demanded. 'I suppose you'd say I was too old to bother with too!'

'Of course not', soothed Ginari. 'Look, Granny, we'll talk about all this tomorrow after the hunt.'

It so happened that 'tomorrow' was too late. With Dingo gone Shontu had no trouble at all tracking the others down. Shortly after the men left, he sneaked up and with great delight swallowed all the women and children whole. He was so pleased with himself that he waddled away singing:

> Haa, haa, haa, hee, hee, hee,
> I'm as happy as can be!
> They went down quick in one big bunch,
> What a yummy, yummy lunch!

When the hunting party returned at dusk they were horrified to find their camp filled with nothing but Shontu's big, fat footprints. They threw themselves on the ground and wailed and wailed.

'We should have listened', sobbed Ginari. 'Granny Wongon was right.' The others nodded their heads sadly in agreement.

'She was such a wonderful person', continued Ginari as tears rolled down his cheeks. 'Because we didn't listen we've lost everything that's important to us.'

'Maybe it's not too late', someone said hopefully.

Ginari brightened. 'What if Granny was right?'

he asked. 'What if there is enough air to keep them alive for a while? There'd be a chance then. That's as long as Shontu is still swallowing things whole and not chewing.'

Desperately clutching any straw, they all leapt up and in the fading light examined the ground closely for any small signs of blood or bone. When they found none they all began to feel much better.

'Let's try to rescue them', said Ginari. 'We've got nothing to lose. The worst that can happen is that he'll eat us too. Then at least we'll all be together!'

Suddenly they all felt braver and more confident. After some discussion they decided the only thing they had going for them was the night. Shontu would be so full that soon he'd be in a deep sleep. If they could somehow open his jaws without disturbing his slumber, they might have a chance. It was a desperate plan for desperate men.

Even in the dark the crocodile wasn't hard to track. The great dollops of dribble he'd left behind wound a shiny, silvery trail through the bush.

'Ssh', said one of the young men as he stopped suddenly. 'What's that noise?'

Burp, whistle, fart!
Burp, whistle, fart!

Their eyes grew large and fearful in the dark as they crept slowly forward. Suddenly in a clearing up ahead they saw a large hill that appeared to be breathing in and out.

They stopped in their tracks at the edge of the clearing.

'What is it?' they whispered to each other as they crept fearfully closer.

'Oh', said Ginari, who was at the front, 'it's Shontu'.

Ginari bravely slid up to Shontu's side, and pressed his frightened ear to the tough skin.

The others stood by wondering if Shontu was really asleep or if he was just pretending.

'Granny Wongon', Ginari whispered as loudly as he dared. 'Can you hear me? Give me a sign if you're still alive.'

A small, angry bump the shape of a finger appeared in the soft skin of Shontu's underbelly. When Ginari saw it he had to stop himself from shouting with joy. His granny was alive, so the chances were that the others would be too.

They all began searching for a dead tree trunk long enough to hold Shontu's jaws open. When they found one strong enough to take the weight they levered it under Shontu's lip, then propped up his top jaw.

Immediately, a strong, putrid gust of swampy air blew up from the crocodile's stomach and knocked them all to the ground. They writhed around, holding their noses and trying not to cough out loud. Ginari was the first to pull himself together. He crawled into Shontu's open mouth and down his throat. He strained his eyes trying to catch sight of any movement in the tunnel, but all he could see was blackness from which came a low rumbling noise.

'Granny, are you still alive?' he called out. 'If that bump wasn't my imagination, please try to come out. We've got Shontu's jaw propped open. Please, Granny, please . . .'

His pleading was interrupted by a sudden rush of creatures stampeding their way to freedom. Ginari had to press himself flat against the side of the crocodile's mouth to avoid being trampled.

The last one out was Granny Wongon and she was cradling a lumpy, limp green creature that looked more dead than alive.

'What's that?' Ginari asked after he had hugged her.

'Dingo!' She smiled proudly. 'I told you he was a good swimmer. He lasted two days.'

Dingo whimpered and dropped his head back on her shoulder. Then his stubby little tail shot bolt upright.

'Dingo's right', said Ginari. 'We'd better get going. It won't be long before Shontu's empty stomach wakes him up.'

That night the family camped deeper in the bush than they had ever done before and held a meeting to try to decide what they could do about Shontu. Granny Wongon fed Dingo a healthy meal and then posted him as lookout. While everyone talked, Dingo paid attention to any strange noise he heard. And every now and then he glanced anxiously at his stubby tail, just to make sure he hadn't missed its signal.

After hours of fruitless discussion they all fell asleep, leaving faithful old Dingo to watch over them until daybreak.

During the night Granny Wongon had a dream. She was swimming in a big pool of water that lay at the base of a tall cliff. The cliff top was bare except for a very large rock, some smaller stones and an old log. She turned her face into the water and saw a giant fish partly embedded in the muddy bottom of the pool. Its face was pointing upwards, as though it was looking for something.

'Dreams!' she muttered the next morning as Dingo woke her with a warm but tired lick. 'Why do they always speak in secrets?'

She felt sure her dream was telling her what to do about Shontu, but although she puzzled over it for days, she couldn't understand it.

Finally, she described the dream to Ginari.

'Well', he said as he scratched his head, 'I don't set much store by dreams myself, but that pool sounds to me like the one Shontu likes to swim in'.

'Of course! Why didn't I think of that? You clever, clever boy', she said as she kissed him. She suddenly understood the dream, including the meaning of the fish. 'My dream has given me a secret weapon. Gather everyone together, we've got work to do!' she cried.

That afternoon, as they all stood nervously by Shontu's favourite pool, they wondered whether the experience of being swallowed had been too much for the old lady. They were sure this was true when she pointed to the cliff and said, 'That's what we have to climb! We're going up there!'

Ginari looked up at the tall, rugged cliff and then down at his very short grandmother, with her spindly legs, blubbery middle and fat flabby bottom. He clamped his teeth together and tried not to laugh.

'You can push me up', she said crossly, realising what he was thinking.

'There's plenty to push on!' giggled one of the children cheekily.

'But why do we have to climb up there?' someone asked.

Granny Wongon glared at them all, found a foothold in the rock and began to climb. She was sick of people not listening to her. Nothing was going to stop her this time!

Ginari rushed after her, frightened she might fall backwards into Shontu's water-hole. The others began to follow slowly. They'd refused to listen to the old lady before and only just lived to regret it. They didn't want to end up in that rancid stomach again.

I don't know what they expected to find when

they reached the top but they were all bitterly disappointed.

'So where's your secret weapon?' Ginari asked when they reached the top.

'Right there!' she said as she pointed to the large rock. Ginari groaned and hoped madness didn't run in the family. The others flopped down on the hard ground complaining. When Granny Wongon saw their reactions she lost her temper.

'I may be old but I'm not stupid!' she shouted. 'You'd all better do exactly as I tell you because it's our last chance!'

After muttering and murmuring among themselves they reluctantly agreed to follow her directions.

They worked in shifts day and night, chiselling patterns into the surface of the rock with sharp flints. It took them a whole week to shape the stone to the old lady's satisfaction. By the end of that week all the food and water they'd brought with them had run out.

'Be patient', Granny Wongon told the children when they complained of hunger and thirst. 'Better an empty stomach and dry throat than no stomach or throat at all! We're nearly finished now.'

When the last pattern was chiselled they used the log to lever the heavy rock over the edge of the cliff. As it fell down into the pool below, a fine spray of cool, clear water shot up and refreshed everyone.

'Just what I needed', sighed the old lady as she laid her aching body on the ground.

'Us too!' the others agreed as they sat down.

'I hope your idea works', said Ginari, 'because if it doesn't, Shontu will have us all!'

'If he comes to eat me again I'm going to close my eyes', said one of the children. 'I hate the way he smiles just before he swallows you.'

'His breath is enough to make you shrivel up and die', Ginari chuckled softly. Soon they were all joking in whispers about Shontu's dreadful manners.

Splash! The Noongals fell silent and looked at each other in alarm. Quickly they peered over the edge of the cliff just in time to see Shontu disappearing into the depths of the blue water.

Shontu was hot and bothered and bad tempered from searching for the Noongals. He wanted to cool off before he began his search again. Never one to miss an opportunity, he swam with his mouth wide open, anxious to catch any fish coming his way. As he glided through the water something caught his eye in the dark depths below. He paused and looked down. What was it? To his enormous pleasure he saw it was a giant fish sleeping on the sandy bottom of the pool.

'Ho, ho, ho', Shontu said to himself eagerly, 'he hasn't even seen me!'

Shontu swooped down, his stomach rumbling hungrily as he plummeted towards the bottom.

The closer Shontu got, the more excited he became. It was one of the biggest fish he'd ever seen. He opened his jaws wider and wider and, with one final lunge, slid them hungrily around his prey.

'It's even bigger than I thought', Shontu sighed happily. He grunted and groaned and wriggled until his catch was tucked safely in the pit of his over-extended belly.

'Aaaah', he smiled contentedly. Then he clamped his jaws tightly together. This was one meal that wasn't going to get away!

He was right, of course! It was impossible for the gigantic stone fish to go anywhere. But what Shontu didn't realise, until it was too late, was that he couldn't go anywhere, either.

# The boy who nearly wished his life away

Yanin couldn't stop wishing. He wished for all sorts of things to happen to himself and other people. He often wished that his sister would turn into a slimy little toad because that's what he thought of her. He wished his grandmother would stop bossing him around. He wished his mother would suddenly gain a beautiful voice so she wouldn't sing out of tune any more, and he wished his father could be shorter so he wouldn't have to look up at him all the time. He wished nice things and nasty things and, sometimes, silly things.

'You'll wish your life away', his sister teased him one day.

'I wish you'd disappear down a bat-hole', he said crossly.

But his sister didn't care. She laughed and ran off chanting:

I wish, I wish, I wish you were a fish,
I'd chop out your gizards, squish, squish, squish!

Yanin looked up at the blue sky and wished it was purple. He examined his toe-nails and wished they were sharp claws. He wished the trees could be red and the earth yellow. He wished birds could bark and snakes could sing. He wished all after-noon until his mother called, 'Tucker time!'

'I wish this was a delicious barramundi', he said as he swallowed a mouthful of watery kangaroo stew.

'I wish you were deaf and dumb', snapped his sister.

Yanin poked his tongue out at her.

'I wish your tongue was a bardi grub', she said nastily.

'It's just as well all our wishes don't come true', sighed their mother. 'I can just imagine the sorts of wishes you'd make for me!'

'Only nice things', said Yanin's sister sweetly.

'What would you wish for me, Yanin?' asked his mother.

Yanin smiled and went on eating. In his mind he'd already wished her to become as fat and round as a wombat, with a nose like an ant-eater and fangs for teeth.

After tea Yanin stretched out and looked up at the night sky. 'I wish I could see in the dark', he sighed. 'And I wish the breeze was warmer and the frogs had long tails and the lizards no legs and . . .'

On and on he wished until he fell into a deep sleep.

Suddenly, Yanin found himself standing on the top of a hill looking down into a valley. As he watched a bird swoop and glide he said, 'I wish I could fly'. In an instant he was shooting upwards at an incredible speed. He flew faster and faster – past birds, past clouds and on through the atmosphere into space.

As Yanin sped on it grew hotter and hotter and the light became brighter and brighter. Within seconds he was as hot as a boiled yam and the sun was racing towards him.

'I don't want to be a charcoal stick', he squeaked as the sun grew larger and larger. 'I wish I could stop flying.'

Back he fell – through the atmosphere, past the clouds and birds, towards the Earth below.

'Aaaarrrgh!' he shrieked when he looked down and realised he was going to land in a bay full of hungry, waiting crocodiles. 'I wish I could float on air.'

He jolted to a halt, his quivering body hovering just out of reach of thirty snapping jaws. He breathed a sigh of relief and lay back and relaxed.

After a while he smiled smugly to himself and said, 'It seems I can get whatever I wish for. Now that I'm used to it, I'm really going to have fun'.

He peered down at the ravenous crocodiles, poked out his tongue and teased, 'Naah, naah, nee, naah, naah! You can't catch me!'

They thrashed around in the water and leapt as high as they could, but he was out of their reach.

It wasn't long before Yanin was bored with floating on air and shouting at crocodiles; he wanted something more exciting to do. As he looked around he noticed a cave just a few metres above the waves. 'I wish I could explore the inside of that cave', he said.

A fierce gust of wind came up and blew him straight in.

The cave was darker than outer space. 'Uh, oh', said Yanin nervously. 'I wish I could see.' The cave lit up. Yanin was standing in front of a giant, human-eating octopus. A long, slimy tentacle flashed towards him, then another and another, until he was completely entangled in their vice-like grip.

'I . . . I . . .', he gasped, but he was so breathless it was difficult to get his wish out. The octopus squeezed him tighter and opened its big, empty mouth. Yanin squeaked in terror, 'I wish I was out of here'.

Before he knew it he was lying among the upper boughs of a tall gum tree. He felt so sick at the thought that he'd nearly been eaten that he said without thinking, 'I wish I was on the ground'.

Thud! He landed on the stony ground.

'Oooh, ooh', he blubbered as he rubbed his bruised bottom. 'Ooh, I wish the ground was softer.' Instantly the soil became softer and softer and Yanin began sinking into it. He flung out his arms to grab hold of a tree root or a rock, but there was none. As the earth sucked him down he choked, 'I wish this was water'.

Water, wonderful water! How good it felt to be able to float and breathe at the same time. He swam and swam. He was having a great time. But he eventually began to tire and realised he was too far away from shore to swim back to land. 'Oh rats!' he cried crossly. 'I wish I had a canoe.'

Within seconds he was lying in the bottom of a small bark canoe. 'Yippee!' he said as he sat up to paddle to shore. But there was no paddle. 'Darn!' he groaned. 'I wish I had a giant paddle so I could get to shore really fast.'

A giant paddle, twenty times the size of the canoe, fell out of the sky and sank everything!

Yanin thrashed angrily in the water once again. It was beginning to dawn on him that wishes weren't as easy to manage as he thought. I'm going to think really hard before I make my next wish, he decided. He began treading water and tried calmly to get his bearings. But his heart jumped a beat when he noticed a small, dark fin breaking through the water in the distance. It turned suddenly and began moving towards him.

'I'm sure it's just a dolphin', Yanin said nervously to himself. But no! That single fin was joined by another and another and the closer they came the more they looked like sharks' fins. The water felt as cold as death. Yanin's teeth chattered noisily as he said, 'I . . . I . . . I wish I was a cannibal shark so I could eat the others up'.

'Eeeek!' squealed Yanin as a large fin grew on his back, his body thickened and his head became pointy and full of razor-sharp teeth. With one huge thrust of his fish-like body he reared up out of the water and began racing towards the other sharks. When they saw how fierce he was they turned and fled. Yanin laughed a horrible, hungry, blood-curdling laugh and thought, I love being a shark! This is the best wish I've made. I'm king of the sea!

He saw a school of gentle dolphins ahead and swam towards them snapping his jaws menacingly. The dolphins took one look at the cannibal shark and darted off in all directions. Yanin laughed another horrible, hungry, blood-curdling laugh and chanted to himself:

I'm a horrible, hungry shark!
My bite is far worse than my bark!
One snap from me and you're history,
I'm a horrible, hungry shark!

He spent the next few hours singing to himself and scaring turtles and jellyfish. In fact, he was having so much fun that without thinking he said, 'I wish I could stay a shark for ever'.

Straight away his blood began to get colder and thinner. His eyes took on a nasty, evil glint. His stomach felt incredibly hungry and he lost his voice. Yanin's wish was coming true. Before he had been a boy in a shark's body, but now he was quickly becoming all shark and no boy.

He spied a school of fish and closed in to swallow them, but suddenly they darted away and disappeared. Yanin the shark was furious. He spun around angrily to see who had scared them off and came face to face with the biggest killer of them all – the giant killer whale.

The whale slowly opened its huge mouth and sucked in the sea-water. Against his will Yanin, the cannibal shark who for a moment had been king of the ocean, moved towards his death. He was overcome with a terrible fear and his last thought was, I . . . I . . . I wish I was home!

With a jolt Yanin opened his eyes. His heart was pounding loudly and he was wet all over.

'Mother, mother!' he cried. 'I'm me, I'm really me! It's so good to be me!'

'Oh Yanin', she said crossly, 'go back to sleep. I wish you had never woken me up'.

'Look! I've got arms', he cried joyfully. 'Two lovely arms! And legs and fingers and toes.' His hands rushed to his head. 'My head is round!' he shouted. 'And I don't have a tail and my blood is warm and I can speak!'

'I wish you couldn't speak', his mother grumbled.

'You don't know what you're saying', he said in horror. 'Never wish anything unless you're absolutely, positively, definitely sure you want it to come true.'

'Well, I know what I want', muttered his sister. 'I wish, I wish, I wish you were a fish . . .'

# The girl who couldn't stop shouting

**M**arni loved the sound of her loud, fiery voice. As a very young child she'd learnt to get her own way simply by shouting. Her whole family gave in to her bad-tempered screams because she could shout louder and longer than anyone they knew. However, the more they gave in to her, the more demanding she became. Eventually she began using her voice for all sorts of awful things, like scaring animals, killing insects and frightening young children.

A wet, hairy caterpillar who foolishly crawled over her foot one day was given a blast from Marni and became completely bald. In fact, the bush was full of deaf goannas, shrivelled up butterflies, featherless birds, and kangaroos who had difficulty hopping straight.

One morning Marni woke up feeling particularly bad tempered. She had over-eaten the night before and had tossed and turned all night. She felt as cross as a Tasmanian devil. And when she opened her mouth to scream and shout she wished she had fangs like one because she really felt like biting somebody.

'Argh!' she howled as she lay on her back on the ground, yelling and kicking. 'Argh, argh, ARGH!'

'What a way to start the day', muttered her mother.

'I'm going', said Marni's grandmother. 'Her voice is worse than thunder!' And she walked off into the bush.

Marni's mother tried to give her daughter something to eat because Marni often screamed for food. But food was the last thing Marni wanted. She spat it out and bit her mother's hand. Then she smiled. She always felt better after she'd bitten someone.

Her mother was a kind person who was far too tolerant of Marni's behaviour. She decided that perhaps her little girl was thirsty, so she gingerly offered her a drink. But Marni became even angrier and sent the water flying. That was the last straw. Her mother walked off to join Granny.

'Whatever happened to that cute, bouncing baby you had?' asked Granny sarcastically when Marni's mother caught up with her.

'She grew up', she sighed.

'We've got to do something about her', Granny said seriously. 'Pythons are still knotted up from her shouting and the frogs are too scared to croak any more. It's got to stop.'

'I know, but what can we do?'

'Magic', said Granny. 'It's the only thing that will work with that child.'

'Not your magic.'

'And what's wrong with my magic?'

'It never works.'

'Of course it works', protested Granny. 'The frogs changed colour, didn't they?'

'But it wasn't the colour they wanted. They don't like being red. And what about the poor kangaroos – it was weeks before their tails grew back.'

'Well, they shouldn't have complained about their tails being heavy', retorted Granny, who liked to take things into her own hands.

'There has to be another way. You're not to do anything until I've had time to think.'

Granny nodded, but she had her fingers very tightly crossed behind her back.

Late that same afternoon, as Marni was stomping angrily through the bush, she suddenly spied her grandmother down near the river. She stopped and crouched down behind a shrub. She didn't want her grandmother to know she was there. Otherwise her shout wouldn't be as effective.

'What a big bum she's got', she said nastily to herself as she watched Granny picking up seeds from the ground. 'She's always complaining about my voice. A splash in the river will do her the world of good and maybe if I'm really lucky, Crocodile will be there, ready for her.'

Marni crept up behind Granny, yelled, and gave her a mighty push.

Much to Marni's delight, Crocodile was ready and waiting. There was a splash and a thrash as Granny and Crocodile wrestled in the water. Despite her meagre strength, Granny managed to cling to the top of Croc's head long enough to get her breath back. She knew magic was the only thing that would save her, so she called out, 'Witchetty grubs'. In an instant she landed wet and bedraggled on the bank, leaving Crocodile still searching for her in the muddy water.

Marni, who had been watching her struggling grandmother with horrible delight, decided it was the right time to leave. She turned and began to run away as fast as her legs could carry her. Granny pointed her middle finger towards the disappearing brat and said breathlessly:

Witchetty grubs and spinifex damper,
Give Crow her noise and Croc her temper.

Make her nice and make her funny,
Make her sweet like wild honey!

As the final words of the spell reached Marni, a terrible feeling came over her. It began in her scalp and flowed all the way down to the tips of her toes. Her insides felt sticky and runny and she wanted to giggle. What was happening to her?

She decided one good, blood-curdling scream would stop her feeling so sickly, so she opened her mouth as wide as she could. Then, with all her might she shouted, but to her horror all that came out was a tiny little sigh.

However, Crow, who was perched in a nearby tree, began to call loudly, 'CAW! CAW! CAW!'

And Crocodile, who had given up searching for Granny, began rolling over and over, thrashing his tail just for the sake of it. For once, Granny's magic had worked!

Marni was so upset at this sudden change in her personality that she turned and began running home as fast as she could. She was nearly there when she saw her mother up ahead carrying a big, fat bungarra over her shoulder. She wanted to screech, 'I hate lizard!', but found herself saying instead, 'Why, Mummy dearest, why don't you let me carry that lovely, juicy bungarra for you?'

Her mother anxiously felt her forehead.

'Are you all right?' she asked.

Marni tried to shout, 'Of course I'm not all right you dill-brain!' but she lovingly said instead, 'You are the sweetest thing to care about me so'.

'You're not all right!' her mother cried. 'Where's Granny?'

Marni and her mother sat down to wait for Granny. Finally, the old lady appeared, looking wet and cross.

'You promised', accused Marni's mother.

'She drove me to it!' protested Granny. And she went on to explain what Marni had done.

'That's a funny story', Marni said, giggling sweetly, when Granny had finished. Granny glared at her angrily. She hated water. Marni kissed her on the cheek, and then picked up the dead bungarra and skipped on ahead of them to prepare dinner.

'My magic does work', said Granny smugly. 'It worked with Croc and now it's worked with Marni, too.'

'Well', sighed Marni's mother. 'I suppose it's all right. Perhaps you're finally getting the hang of it.'

When Marni's father and brother returned from their hunting trip late that night Marni leapt up and made them something to eat.

'There you are Daddy darling and beautiful Brother', she cooed as she kissed their cheeks. 'I'll see your lovely faces in the morning.'

Both Daddy darling and beautiful Brother were shocked into silence. Where had their bad-tempered brat gone? They looked suspiciously in Granny's direction, but she was pretending to be asleep.

In the morning Granny told Marni's father that the change was for the better. 'She won't frighten off the game any more', said Granny proudly. 'You can hunt close to home now.'

Everyone was happy with this thought. Marni began to giggle.

Unfortunately, as the day wore on, Marni grew sillier and sillier.

When her grandmother stubbed her toe she chortled sweetly:

> Granny, Granny in the dirt
> How much does your big toe hurt?

And when her brother accidentally broke his spear she giggled:

> Brother, brother you're so slick
> Broke a spear and made a stick.

By the end of the day she was driving everyone crazy with her silly, giggly sayings.

'We've got to do something about her', Granny sighed that night.

'That's what you said before you changed her', retorted Marni's mother.

'I don't care how horrible she was before', said

her father, 'if she calls me Daddy darling once more I'll be sick!'

'It's up to you, Granny', said beautiful Brother. 'It's your magic.'

'But that's just the trouble', she sighed. 'It's not *all* my magic any more. Crow and Crocodile share it now. Unless they agree to give her voice and temper back, I can't do a thing.'

Just then Marni giggled in her sleep and they all looked desperately at Granny.

'All right, all right', she said. 'I'll see what I can do in the morning!'

Early the next morning Granny walked down to the river and called, 'Crocky, Crocky, are you there?'

'Push off you wrinkly old bag', a very cross voice replied.

'Come on, Crocky', she coaxed. 'I've been good to you over the years and I've forgiven you for trying to eat me. I know it was just your instincts coming out.'

Crocodile poked his very large head out of the water and said grumpily, 'What is it?'

'I want my granddaughter's bad temper back.'

'NO! NO! NO!' he snapped. 'Everyone is terrified of me now.'

'What about just a little bit of it then?' Granny bargained.

'NO!'

'Crocky', she said slyly, 'if you stay that nasty,

the things you like to eat won't come anywhere near you. You'll starve to death'.

'Oh no!' bellowed Crocky, who loved a varied menu. 'All right, just a little.'

Granny pointed her middle finger at him and held out the empty palm of her other hand.

'Witchetty grugs!' she said, and in an instant Croc had disappeared back under the water and in her hand was a tiny red seed.

It wasn't hard for Granny to find Crow because she could hear his raucous voice.

'Crow', she shouted as she stood under the tree he was sitting in. 'Can you hear me?'

'CAW!' he screeched.

'Don't talk, just listen', she begged. 'I want my granddaughter's noise back.'

Crow flew up to a higher branch and shook his head. 'I'm louder than Kookaburra now', he shouted. 'I love being the noisiest bird in the bush.'

'But, Crow', she replied, 'if you stay that noisy, you'll frighten away those lovely fat grubs you like to eat'.

'CAAAAW!' he screamed angrily. 'All right, you can have a little bit. But I still want to stay a loud bird.'

Granny performed her magic rite once more, only this time a tiny black seed appeared in her hand. After that she happily went home.

'But why can't I have *all* my noise and *all* my

temper back?' Marni demanded after she'd swallowed the seeds.

'You're lucky to get what you did, my girl', said Granny firmly. 'And let this be a warning to you. I'm sure Crow and Crocodile would be happy to help me out again.'

Marni smiled, then curled her hands into two fists. She jumped up and down, went red in the face and opened her mouth wide. 'Argh!' she shrieked. But to everyone's relief, only a medium-sized 'argh' came out. From then on, thanks to Granny, Marni was only noisy and bad tempered now and then. Crow is still one of the loudest birds in the bush, and Crocodile is still so bad tempered that he eats all that comes his way.

# The first white man

**W**adjella lived with his mother, father, two older brothers, grandmother and various aunts, uncles and cousins near a large lake. In the deepest, darkest part of the lake, down in the slippery, slimy mud, lived Munka, a giant fish. This huge fish was an ancient creature who had earned great respect because everyone knew how greedy he was. Each night at midnight he rose up to the surface of the water to hunt. 'Food!' he would roar loudly as he thrust his great big fish head up through the water. 'I want food!'

His greedy, bulging eyes looked ready to pop out and devour whatever they saw. And his spiky, razor-sharp teeth were always sharpening them-selves against one another in hungry anticipation.

Munka would have emptied the lake of its fish and turtles long ago if it hadn't been for the sleeping spell one of Wadjella's ancestors had cast over it. The great fish liked to feed day and night and when he had almost emptied the lake of all life he began to swallow people and animals; in short anything silly enough to come close to the water. Once the spell was cast, however, the lake became a safe place dur-ing the day because Munka could now only hunt between midnight and sunrise. The rest of his time was spent in a deep sleep on the murky bottom.

When Wadjella was very young his mother had taught him a rhyme so he'd never be tempted to wander around the lake at the wrong time. It went like this:

When darkness falls and the sky is black,
And the stars all blink with fright,
Munka comes up with his open mouth
In the middle of the night.
'Food!' he screams. 'I want food! Any child will do!
I'll snap him up and crunch his bones and grind him
    into stew!'

As you can imagine, that rhyme gave Wadjella terrible nightmares. He often dreamt he was being eaten alive or floating in pieces in Munka's stomach, surrounded by smelly, old fish heads and shredded turtle necks.

As Wadjella grew older he tried not to think too much about Munka. He could even manage several days in a row where the thought of the fish didn't bother him at all. However, whenever he began to relax his grandfather would tell him another horrifying story, or his mother would recite the different names of past relatives who'd been eaten.

However, by the time he was a teenager he was beginning to wonder if the story of Munka was anything more than a silly old legend. He had spent his childhood in dread of a fish he'd never seen. No one he actually knew had been attacked, let alone eaten. Of course, occasionally at midnight he'd heard a dim roar coming from the lake, but he was sure this was simply the wind tearing through the thick canopy of the trees.

Now Wadjella didn't consider there to be much difference between being a teenager and being a man. He liked to think of himself as brave and adventurous. Although he was thin, he was quite a fast runner. And his father often told him that one day he would be a great hunter. He was exceptionally good at making fish traps, and often supplied his mother with a fresh, juicy fish to cook for the family's tea. Young girls who lived in the area soon heard about him and began to pay him exaggerated compliments, hoping for a fish for themselves. Unfortunately, Wadjella believed every word they said, and he became vain, boastful and overbearing.

His claims of bravery and skill grew wilder and wilder until he began calling himself the greatest hunter who ever lived. His cousins became heartily sick of him because he always found a way to outdo them, even if it meant cheating.

One day, as Wadjella stood flexing his arm muscles and thinking about how strong he was, one of his younger cousins saw him and called out, 'You think you're really something, don't you!'

'I am', replied Wadjella, who was trying to decide whether to thump the boy or not.

'You're weak!' his cousin retorted. Wadjella's eyes narrowed in anger, but as he reached out to grab his cousin the boy darted away chanting, 'Weak, weak, weak!'

Soon the younger boy was joined by an older cousin who began chanting the same thing. Wadjella would have liked to beat them up, but the older boy was taller, so he decided to play it cool instead.

'I am tough!' he yelled at them. 'You ask me to do anything, anything at all, and I'll do it!'

The boys whispered quickly to one another and then the older one said, 'We dare you to go to the lake at midnight and catch Munka then!'

Both of the cousins were terrified of the fish

and they presumed Wadjella would be the same. They were amazed when he stuck out his chest and replied confidently, 'No worries! I'm not afraid of going to the lake at midnight and catching any old fish that turns up.'

The cousins ran off laughing uneasily, but they didn't really think he'd be foolish enough to go anywhere near Munka.

However, Wadjella believed he was a great enough hunter to catch a giant fish. He didn't for a moment believe that Munka – if he existed at all – could be as fierce as the stories made out. Wadjella took the dare very seriously and spent the rest of his day making the biggest fish trap he'd ever attempted from twine and wood. Then towards sunset he dragged it down and placed it in the lake near the exact spot where his mother maintained Munka had last been seen.

Late that night, when everyone was asleep, Wadjella crept silently away from the camp. He reached the lake just before midnight and sat down confidently on the damp ground. He gripped his father's best spear tightly. He'd brought it just for luck. He didn't really think he'd need it. 'No worries', he kept muttering as he patted the spear. 'No worries at all.'

Wadjella didn't know whether it was his imagination or not, but there seemed to be an eerie atmosphere about the lake. As he watched the slow, smooth ripples on the surface of the water, he kept seeing skulls with big, empty holes where eyes had once been. And when he looked at the moonlit outline of the trees he imagined thin, white, skeleton-like arms were reaching out to grab him. He shivered. The air seemed to have grown very chilly and still. That breeze is as cold as death, he thought as he rubbed his feet together.

Then suddenly a very strong wind blew in out of nowhere and began howling around the trees. Wadjella was sure he could hear his mother's voice howling with the wind:

> When darkness falls and the sky is black,
> And the stars all blink with fright,
> Munka comes up with his open mouth
> In the middle of the night.
> 'Food!' he screams. 'I want food.
> Any child will do!
> I'll snap him up and crunch his bones
>    and grind him into stew!'

He gulped hard as a sudden terrible thought occurred to him. What if Munka really existed? What if he was as fierce as everyone said?

'Food!' a great, ugly brute roared as it thrust its huge, slimy head out of the water. 'I want food! Any child will do! I'll snap him up and crunch his bones and grind him into stew.'

Wadjella's heart leapt into his mouth as his

eyes focused on the terrible, serrated teeth before him.

'I want food!' the monster screamed again as it peered angrily through the shattered remains of Wadjella's trap. Wadjella's mouth began to quiver uncontrollably with fear, and his teeth knocked together like loose knuckle-bones when the monster eyeballed him.

'So you're the horrible, evil boy who set that measly trap! I'll have you in bits in no time at all!'

Wadjella tried desperately to beg for mercy, but the only sound he made was a hoarse little 'Eeeeeeh'. Munka had no pity. He reared up out of the water and opened his cavernous mouth. In one terrifying moment the boy was sucked inside Munka's huge jaws.

Fortunately for Wadjella he was skinny enough to pass through Munka's mouth without touching the razor-sharp teeth. He tried to halt his backward slide down the fish's smelly throat, but there was nothing for him to cling to. He closed his eyes and hoped the end would come quickly.

To his utter surprise, his slippery slide suddenly stopped. He opened his eyes and saw that his father's spear, which he had been tightly gripping all this time, had become lodged in a fleshy part of the throat. Wadjella clung on for dear life. He didn't fancy being dissolved by the red stomach acid that was bubbling up to meet him.

Again and again the great fish tried to swallow,

but each time he gagged instead. In the end he choked violently and vomited Wadjella and the spear back onto the bank.

'I want flesh, not bone!' Munka roared furiously. And with one huge, bad-tempered thrash of his dark tail he swam off to look for something fat.

Wadjella lay on the bank as weak as a jellyfish. He was sick with fear. I'll never boast about anything again, he thought. Slowly his strength began to return and he started to feel he might soon be able to move. He relaxed his arms and legs and stretched out his hands and fingers. 'One, two, three, four, five', he counted on each hand. Yes, they were all there. He sat up and wriggled his toes. There were five on each foot. How wonderful. He couldn't believe he'd come through his ordeal whole.

But that's funny, he thought suddenly as he glanced at himself in the moonlight. He brought his hand right up to his face and examined his skin.

'Argh!' he gasped. He'd gone white with fright. He was lily white from the top of his head to the tip of his toes.

And that is how the first white man came into the world.

# Roly poly
# the wombat

Roly Poly the wombat squeezed out of his burrow and sniffed the sweet, clear air. His nose twitched and his nostrils widened as he breathed deeply.

'Aah', he sighed. 'The first day of spring, my favourite time of the year!' Roly Poly smiled as he thought of what spring meant to him. The weather was beautiful: not too hot and not too cold. Just warm enough to feel comfortable and contented. He loved the newness of spring and the way everything seemed to be reborn, himself included. And there was no shortage of food during spring, either. But, best of all, the girl wombats were very friendly. Roly Poly blushed at the thought.

A brightly coloured butterfly fluttered down and landed gently on his nose. Roly Poly watched it dreamily. Butterflies were so beautiful. They made him feel very romantic. I wonder whom I'll meet today, he thought shyly. But his daydreaming was rudely interrupted by a loud rumble from his stomach. 'Oh dear', said Roly Poly. 'Before I think about anything else I had better find some food.'

Soon he was munching on some deliciously moist leaves. The more he ate, the hungrier he realised he was. There was nothing like spring for giving you a good appetite. Greedily, he swallowed mouthful after mouthful.

Now, watching the happy wombat from the lower branch of a nearby tree was Magpie, who was in a very bad mood and looking for someone to pick on.

'Hey, fatso', he called out nastily. 'You look like a fat, flat rock from up here!'

Roly Poly ignored him and went on eating. Everyone knew just how cantankerous magpies could be. It was best not to reply because they only became worse and worse.

But this magpie was really cross and didn't like being ignored. He flew down and landed on the grass next to Roly Poly.

'Did you hear me, fatso?' he asked nastily. 'Or are you deaf as well as dumb? No answer, eh? All right, well I'll tell you just what I think of you! If you were any fatter your fur would roll over your eyes and you wouldn't be able to find food or a springtime girlfriend!'

Roly Poly blushed furiously but went on eating.

'You wombats think you're so good at finding food and girlfriends', said Magpie. 'Well, you might be right about that, but what girl would want a tub of lard!' And with that Magpie flew off, feeling much better.

When Magpie was gone, Roly Poly moved his little eyes from side to side and up and down and round and round.

'Silly old Magpie', he said. 'I can see whatever I want to. He just wants to spoil my day, but I'm not going to let him!' He began eating again, but Magpie's comment about no girls liking him stayed in his mind. He began to wonder if it might be true.

A soft breeze wafted by, filled with the fragrance of fresh green grass. The wombat paused. He'd nearly eaten all the leaves anyway, so he decided to follow his nose and move on. He found some grass in a clearing near the river and settled down among the damp blades to eat to his heart's content.

After a while Shiny Black Beetle scurried past chirruping:

I'm sleek and shiny and made to go,
You're fat and hairy and ever so slow!

Roly Poly choked. What was wrong with everyone today. It was spring, didn't they know that?

He looked at as much of himself as was possible and said to himself, 'I'm not that fat. I'm just a normal wombat size'. A depressing picture of a girl wombat calling him a fatso suddenly flashed into his mind. He closed his eyes and sighed a deep sigh. Then he opened his mouth again and went on eating. The grass was unbelievably delicious and it made him feel a little better. This is a good place, he thought as he pulled up another tuft of grass. If I stay here all day I might meet someone who likes to eat as much as I do.

He was right, it was a good place to meet someone. But if Roly Poly could have known what was creeping up the river-bank he would have scurried away as fast as his short little legs could carry him. It was Crocodile!

'Oooh, I'm hungry!' Crocodile said to himself. 'There's not enough fish to eat in the river, I need something really filling.' He stopped and sniffed and then he turned his head in the direction of meat. 'Somewhere near here', he drooled, 'is fat wombat! I can smell it! A big, round, solid bit of meat', he chuckled delightedly to himself. 'What a treat!'

Roly Poly was so busy eating and thinking

about how he could get girl wombats to like him that he did not hear Crocodile's rumbling stomach. 'I don't care what she's like', he said dreamily to himself. 'I haven't met a wombat yet that wasn't wonderful!'

When Crocodile first glimpsed Roly Poly he thought about how delicious wombats could be. He crept up behind his prey and said in a quiet, hungry voice, 'Hellooo, fatso! How lovely you are!'

Roly Poly turned and squeaked in fear at Crocodile's gaping jaws. He began to waddle away furiously.

The sight of Roly Poly's retreating, wobbling backside was so funny that it made Crocodile pause. 'You idiot', he laughed. 'Have you forgotten that I can run even faster than a human on land?'

Roly Poly hadn't forgotten. But he didn't care how fast Crocodile could run, all he could think of was that he had to get away. A lot of horrible things had happened to him that day and an even worse thing was about to happen if he didn't escape!

Crocodile's amusement overcame his hunger as he gazed at the wombat trying to run.

'I wouldn't mind having a play before I chomp on him', he muttered to himself. 'It might make him more tender.' Crocodile caught up with Roly Poly and walked close behind him, trying to imitate his waddle. Now and then he snapped his jaws very close to the wombat's rear end, making Roly Poly jump with fright.

'I just can't believe it', Roly Poly puffed as his run became more frenzied. 'This has to be the worst spring of my life!'

Suddenly, Shiny Black Beetle who had teased him earlier scuttled past. I wish I was made to go fast, thought the terrified Roly Poly.

Shiny Black Beetle squeaked, 'You'd both better run faster than that. Mean old Moola has a new recipe for his dinner and it's got beetle and magpie and crocodile and wombat in it!'

The mention of Moola's name was enough to terrify everyone. Moola was an insanely greedy giant who had recently come to live in Australia. He showed no mercy when it came to catching the ingredients for his meals!

Crocodile snapped his jaws for the last time and zapped past Roly Poly and Shiny Black Beetle. It was one thing for him to eat, but quite another to be eaten. Not even a creature of his size and strength was a match for Moola.

Roly Poly continued to run on, trying to keep up with Shiny Black Beetle and Crocodile ahead of him. He puffed and panted and heaved, but he was so round and fat he felt like he was dragging a big, heavy rock with him. 'I am ever so slow', he moaned, as Shiny Black Beetle and Crocodile disappeared out of sight.

He was just about to drop when Magpie flew

past screeching, 'Run faster, fatso! Moola's not far behind and his recipe's got beetle, crocodile, magpie and wombat in it!'

There was a loud roar. Roly Poly nearly jumped out of his hot, sweaty skin when he heard it. He glanced over his shoulder and saw Moola with his Magic Pouch. The giant was so tall he had clouds floating around his head. Roly Poly winced as a huge dollop of dribble landed near him. He was so scared that little noises began to come from his mouth, and his nostrils pinched themselves together in fright.

'I've got a new recipe!' shouted Moola. 'And it's got beetle and crocodile and magpie and fat, fat wombat in it!'

Roly Poly looked up ahead and saw the others had abruptly halted in their flight. He realised that they had stupidly run in the direction of a cliff. No one could go any further.

'Fly!' Roly Poly called breathlessly to Magpie. 'At least you can get away.' But Magpie was frozen with fear. His wings hung limply at his side. He wasn't going anywhere.

With a final spurt of speed Roly Poly shot towards the others. However, he ran so fast he couldn't control his tired little legs any longer. He hurtled over the cliff and fell down, down, down towards the thick bushes below.

Moola scooped the others up and put them in his Magic Pouch. Then he peered downwards to the base of the cliff, hunting for Roly Poly. 'Hmph!' he finally snorted when he couldn't find him. 'I want fat wombat, not flat wombat!' And he angrily stormed away.

Roly Poly slowly opened his small eyes and blinked. He couldn't see. I'm dead, he thought. But then he realised it was only dark because he was under the bushes. He inspected his fat, hairy body all over and when he saw he was all there he said in astonishment, 'My fat saved me! It cushioned my fall!'

There was a loud, snuffling noise nearby. He went very quiet in case Moola was still looking for him. He watched nervously as a nose poked out from under the bush next to him. It twitched, breathed deeply and then sniffed. Something made the sound of a contented sigh and through the tangle of leaves and branches squeezed a very fat, round, hairy wombat. 'Well, hellooo cuddles!' she said when she saw Roly Poly.

'Maybe I am in heaven', he whispered as she shuffled up to him. 'This really is the best time of the year!'

# The proud goanna

Goanna was the proudest animal in the bush. One bright morning he came out of his burrow feeling particularly fine. As he haughtily looked around, his long tongue flicked in and out: a sign that he was feeling very alert. He was hungry and keen to find something to eat.

'Hello, Goanna', said Python, who was lying sleepily on a dead tree trunk in the sun.

Goanna looked at him and said, 'I'm glad I'm not as low to the ground as you are, Python. You must feel every bump and stone. My short legs are very strong and take me everywhere I want to go'.

'Ssssss', said Python and promptly went back to sleep.

Feeling very proud of his sturdy legs, Goanna trotted off through the bush to look for food. He held his head up just a little, as if to say, 'Aren't I something!'

'Hello, Goanna', said Numbat. 'Are you hunting for food too?'

'Yes', replied Goanna. 'And I NEVER have any trouble finding it. My eyes are sharp and quick to spot tasty things in the bush.' Then he looked at Numbat and said, 'I'm glad I don't have fur like yours, Numbat. I bet all sorts of twigs and bugs get stuck in it and make you itchy. My skin is sleek and tough, nothing sticks to it'.

Numbat rolled his eyes and sprinted off.

Feeling very proud of his sharp eyesight and smooth skin, Goanna continued his search for food, and, as he walked, he held his head just a little bit higher as if to say, 'I really am something!'

'Hello, Goanna', said Wombat as he snuffled in the dirt. 'Have you had breakfast yet?'

'Not yet', replied Goanna. 'But I will soon. Goannas are good hunters.' Then he looked at Wombat and said, 'I'm glad I'm not fat like you, Wombat. You run so slowly and look so silly. I bet you get stuck in lots of places. I'm slim and quick. I can fit just about anywhere!'

Wombat grunted and waddled off. He knew better than to argue with Goanna, the proudest animal in the bush.

Goanna thought he would hunt for food down near the river, and, feeling very proud of his slim build, he held his head even higher as he walked, as if to say, 'I'm sooo good!'

'Hello, Goanna', said Crocodile, who was floating log-like in the water. 'You're looking very fine this lovely sunny morning.'

Goanna smiled, gazed down at Crocodile and replied, 'I'm glad I'm not like you, Crocodile. Your body is so big and awkward and your skin is all wrinkled from lying in the water all day. I'm sleek and smooth, slim and strong. I have sharp eyesight, tough legs and flat, beautiful scales'.

Crocodile smiled his usual smile and replied, 'You're right, Goanna. You're all those things, and more! You deserve to be proud. What I like best is the way you hold your head high in the air as you walk along. Why, I bet all the other animals think of you as Top Goanna!'

At this compliment Goanna's neck stretched out as far as possible. So far, in fact, that he could hardly talk.

'Thank you', he squeaked as he held his head high.

'Oh, that's perfect!' replied Crocodile. 'What a sight you are, Goanna. You just keep walking along like that and everyone who sees you will be very impressed.'

Goanna managed a tiny smile. It really was very difficult holding his head high but, as Crocodile said, he did look good.

Goanna walked slowly over to the warm, flat rock that was lodged high over the river-bed. 'I'm Top Goanna', he hummed.

Suddenly Goanna's strong, short legs were treading air. The rock beneath him had finished. His head had been held so high, he hadn't noticed.

Down, down, down the proudest animal in the bush fell – right into a pair of waiting jaws below. With a snap and a gulp he was gone. Crocodile floated log-like on his way again.

'Sleek and meaty', he said to himself. 'Slim enough to swallow whole, a tasty snack that fits in even when one is full!'

# The gourmet giant

**M**oola wasn't just any old giant, he was an enormous giant with an enormous appetite to match. He roamed throughout the world tasting all the gourmet delights it had to offer. In Africa his favourite meal had been Boiled Tiger Tails in Honey-ant Sauce. In France he had loved the Roasted Frog Stomachs with Slimy Green Moss Side Salad. And in Tibet he had raved about Cat's Eyes Dipped in Melted Chicken Liver. He had an insatiable appetite for new dishes and he stored hundreds of ingredients for these in a magic pouch.

After travelling around the world several times he finally decided to settle in Australia. One taste was enough to convince him that Australia had the best food in the world. He was delighted with the wonderful flavour of Roast Witchetty Grubs basted in Mashed Magpie Brain Sauce. He couldn't wait to nibble a Tasmanian tiger, bite into a duck-billed platypus and munch on a numbat.

Now, Moola wasn't simply addicted to trying new flavours. He would, in fact, only eat the same dish once. He became very upset if it was suggested that he eat the same thing twice. But as everyone knows there is a limited supply of different foods, and that was what eventually caused the trouble.

'Poor old me, poor old me!' Moola cried one day as he sat in Australia hugging his empty bowl. He'd just finished scraping up the last remnants of Casserole of Cockatoo Tail and Bull-ant Legs. 'Poor old me, poor old me!' he wailed over and over. 'I've travelled the world and eaten a little and a lot of everything, and now there's nothing left to try. Oh, poor old me!'

'More like poor old me!' complained Nardu, who was his human cook and longstanding companion. 'I spend all day cooking and cleaning, collecting firewood and inventing new recipes – all you have to do is eat them.' Nardu was fed up with Moola's appetite. He wished he was interested in some-thing besides food.

Moola sniffed loudly. 'Food is my life', he said and he burst into tears again at the mention of the word food. 'There must be something I haven't eaten', he sighed when he finally stopped crying. He began to wipe his wet face with his tongue and muttered, 'If I can't eat new things I might as well be dead!' For the next hour he sat silently with his head in his hands. It was late afternoon and the sun was just beginning to set. Nardu stretched out on the ground beside him, relieved that the noise had finally stopped. They lay quietly and watched the sun sink slowly behind the horizon.

'I've got it!' Moola suddenly shouted, so loudly that Nardu leapt up in fright.

'What did you say?' he asked.

'I said', repeated the giant, 'that I've got it!' He spoke very distinctly and smiled very slowly, and a strange, scary glint appeared in his eyes. Nardu gulped. For no apparent reason he suddenly felt frightened. Moola's look reminded him of a hungry python ready to strike.

'I . . . I'll make you some Pickled Snake-head Soup', Nardu offered quickly.

'I had that the other week', replied the giant. 'What I want is something new and I think I've just thought of it.' A thin line of dribble rolled out of the corner of his mouth and down his chin.

'N . . . n . . . not me!' stuttered Nardu.

'Not you, you old fool', Moola roared as he picked him up by one leg and examined him closely. 'You're too stringy and bony. I want something tender and innocent.'

'So you don't mean humans then?' Nardu sighed with relief as the giant dropped him back on the sand.

'Of course I mean humans', Moola replied, 'but not just any humans – fat, juicy babies are what I want!;'

'You monster!' stormed Nardu. 'You human-eating . . .'

'Oh, cut out the compliments', snapped Moola as he turned him upside down in the sand so he couldn't protest any more. 'I'm going to sleep. Tomorrow I gather babies in my magic pouch, and I expect you to have a new recipe ready. Do you hear me?'

Nardu pulled his head out of the soft ground and nodded. He couldn't say much because his mouth was still full of sand.

The giant lay down and began to snore happily. Nardu spat out the sand and eyed Moola in disgust. He was very upset by the giant's latest idea. Moola had been growing meaner and meaner as the years went by. Nardu remembered when the giant had been generous and friendly. But that was before food had become his life's obsession.

'What can I do to stop him?' he said to himself. He'd been with Moola long enough to know the giant wouldn't stop at babies. When he got bored with them he'd start eating children, then men and women. Why, the time might come when he wouldn't consider Nardu old and stringy at all!

If only I could get hold of his Magic Pouch, I might be able to do something, Nardu thought. The Magic Pouch was very powerful. It could talk and feel but it could never leave the giant while he lived. Only Moola's hands could open it and if anybody else tried to touch the Magic Pouch it would cry out. And woe betide any person caught with Moola's Magic Pouch in his hands.

'There are only two things that can get near that pouch safely', muttered Nardu to himself. 'Moola, or a juicy, innocent baby!'

Nardu straightened suddenly as an idea occurred to him. What if he could somehow disguise himself as a baby? Then the giant would put him inside the Magic Pouch and perhaps he'd be able to use its magic. Nardu thought and thought. It seemed impossible – to look like a baby he'd need magic, but he had none. Then he remembered that when they'd first come to Australia he'd seen an unusually large bee hiding among some Sturt's desert peas. He'd thought at the time that it must be a magic bee because it was about six centimetres long and was pink and scarlet. It was the only one of its kind he'd seen in the whole world. If he could find that bee, he decided, it just might be able to help him!

Nardu left the sleeping giant and wandered through the bush in search of the bee. He wished he could speak bee language. 'Buzz, buzz, buzz', he called out, trying to sound like a bee. 'Buzz, buzz, buzz.'

After buzzing around for over an hour with no reply he decided it might help if he mimicked other things bees did, like flapping their wings and sniffing flowers. He bent over to make himself look smaller, moved his arms in a flying motion and sniffed at flowers in the pale moonlight.

The Magic Bee, who'd been watching all along, couldn't contain her laughter any more. She flew from the tree she was hiding in to a nearby bush and said, 'Oh, do stop, you silly man, and tell me what it is you want!'

Nardu felt very embarrassed. He stopped buzzing and dropped his hands to his sides.

'I need your help', he told the bee meekly.

'Moola is your friend and you need my help?' asked the incredulous Magic Bee.

'That's why I need your help', said Nardu sadly. 'He was a good giant once, but he's changed. All that strange food he's eaten has made him strange. All he thinks about are his taste-buds. And now he even wants to eat tender, innocent babies!'

'I can see you're in a sticky situation', said the Magic Bee cautiously. She wasn't sure whether to take him seriously or not. 'But what makes you think I can help?'

'I've been everywhere', replied Nardu, 'and I've never seen a bee like you before. You must have magic in you'.

The Magic Bee smiled proudly. This human was obviously brighter than he looked.

'Turn me into a baby', pleaded Nardu, 'the fattest, juiciest baby in the whole world. Then the giant will put me in his Magic Pouch to eat'.

I was wrong, thought the Magic Bee. He's as thick as a tree trunk!

'Tell me', she buzzed in an amused way. 'Have you wanted to be eaten for long?'

'Of course not!' replied Nardu. 'It's only a new idea! You're not taking me seriously.'

The Magic Bee shook her small head in confusion. Either this man deserved to be eaten or she was missing something.

'But why do you want to be eaten?' she asked. She was beginning to feel annoyed by his stupidity.

'I don't want to be eaten!' shouted Nardu. 'I just want to get inside the Magic Pouch. Once I'm in there I might be able to use its magic to stop Moola's revolting plans.'

'I zeeeee', sighed the Magic Bee. 'You'll be taking a terrible risk. Isn't there any other way you can get the giant to beehive himself?'

Nardu groaned loudly. This was no time for jokes. The Magic Bee must have thought twice about her remark for she apologised and said, 'All right, I'll help you. If Moola is as bad as you say, none of us is safe. I'll not only turn you into a baby; I'll give you two weapons as well'.

The Magic Bee wiggled and made a high-pitched sound. Immediately, a small piece of bright yellow honeycomb and a single star appeared in Nardu's empty hand.

'What can I use these for?' Nardu asked, almost ungratefully. He was thinking how useless a star and a bit of honeycomb were against a giant.

'If a good person eats the honeycomb', answered the Magic Bee, 'he will say it tastes bitter, but an evil person will say it's the sweetest thing he's ever tasted. For all its bitterness it will reward a good person, but it will curse an evil person in spite of its sweetness'.

Before Nardu could ask about the star, the Magic Bee flew down and stung him on the nose. Nardu found himself transformed into the fattest, juiciest baby in the whole world and whizzing through the air back to where Moola was snoring. He landed heavily next to Moola's Magic Pouch, where he lay on his tummy and began to coo quietly.

When Moola finally woke it was bright sunlight. He yawned, picked his giant nose and sat up. (Just in case you're wondering, that was one thing he'd tasted over and over again.) He sniffed deeply. What was that he could smell? He sniffed again.

'Baby!' he roared hungrily. 'I smell baby!'

'WAA!' screamed the Baby, who, even though he was really a man, couldn't help being frightened.

Moola's nose quickly discovered the baby. The giant scooped him up eagerly and placed him stomach down on the palm of his hand.

'I'm so lucky', he said greedily. 'I've found the fattest, juiciest baby in the whole world without even looking. And it's mine, all mine!' He popped the Baby quickly into his Magic Pouch, then yelled, 'Nardu, get the fire ready!'

When Nardu failed to appear Moola roared again and again. In the end hunger drove him to collect the firewood himself.

Meanwhile, inside the pouch, the fattest, juiciest baby in the whole world rolled over and over sucking his thumb, gurgling and puzzling over where the pouch's magic came from. Just when he thought he'd never work it out a voice like rushing water sang:

> Bitter is to sweet as sweet is to bitter,
> To catch a giant make the bait glitter.

'Goo', said the baby in response. 'Goo, goo.' But what did the rhyme mean, he wondered, as he chewed hungrily on his fist.

Fortunately for the Baby the pouch grew tired of waiting for him to work it out and said, 'Do you have any bait?'

'Waa', cried the Baby in fright. 'Waa, waa!'

The Magic Pouch sighed and waited patiently for him to stop screaming. Finally, the Baby stopped blubbering and patted himself on the head instead, indicating to the pouch that he thought he was the bait.

'Fat and stupid', the Magic Pouch muttered to itself. 'Just when I want to get away from Moola, look what I'm stuck with!'

Very slowly and clearly, so the stupid Baby could understand, the Magic Pouch asked, 'What do you have that is bitter and sweet?'

The Baby held up the honeycomb. As he looked at it he thought it was so nice he wouldn't mind having a suck.

'Clever boy!' said the Magic Pouch. 'You finally got something right. Now, what do you have that glitters?'

The Baby's face went blank. Then he began screaming and holding out an empty hand. After that he pointed to his toothless gums. The Magic Pouch groaned. It realised that the Baby was trying to communicate that he had nothing that glittered, not even teeth.

'And to think all humans start off like this', said the Magic Pouch to itself in amazement. Aloud it said, 'Shut up! You're being a naughty boy! If you don't stop I'll pinch your honeycomb'.

The Baby gave a final, loud snort and hugged the honeycomb to his plump little body. Then he poked out his bottom lip and sulked.

'Stop that sulking!' said the Magic Pouch, who was feeling very frustrated. 'My magic tells me there's a man inside those rolls of fat somewhere, so listen carefully and for heaven's sake stop peeing on me!'

'Goo', said the Baby in as adult a manner as possible.

'Nothing glitters more than a star', explained the Magic Pouch slowly. The Baby nodded in agreement.

Boy, he's dumb, thought the Magic Pouch. He's forgotten he's got the star!

'If you'll roll over', said the Magic Pouch patiently, 'you'll find you're lying on a star'.

The Baby rolled over onto his back, farting as he did so. The Magic Pouch coughed and fervently hoped this ridiculous situation would be over soon.

The Baby found the star, picked it up and began admiring its shiny shape.

Just then the giant returned and dropped his load of firewood near the Magic Pouch. The Baby began to scream in terror. But the Magic Pouch managed to quieten him long enough to say, 'Quickly, smear the honey from the honeycomb over the star. It's our only chance!'

The Baby did as he was told and, to his amazement, although the star continued to glitter, it also began to smell like the best thing in the whole world.

'When Moola is taken care of', added the Magic Pouch, 'promise to take me with you. I'm sick of belonging to greedy, grumpy giants'.

'Goo', agreed the baby.

When the roaring fire had died down to red-hot coals the enormous giant opened his pouch.

'WAA!' cried the baby in fear. 'WAA! WAA!'

'I'd better eat you before I go deaf', said Moola as he licked his lips.

In desperation the Baby held up the star and to his utter surprise a change began to come over the giant. He stopped licking his lips. His eyes lost their glazed, meaty look and he smiled a far-away, dreamy sort of smile.

'Mmmmmm', he slurped as he gazed at the tiny star. 'Mmmmm, mmmmm!'

For some reason he couldn't understand, he no longer wanted the fattest, juiciest baby in the whole world. He wanted the star instead. He took the star from the Baby's fat little hand and gently placed it in his own mouth.

'Ooooh', he sighed. 'It's so very, very sweet.'

'Gooo', said the Baby. 'Gooo, gooo!'

The Magic Pouch groaned. He thought the Baby was laying it on a bit thick.

'As sweet, as sweet, as sweeeet!' hummed Moola, who suddenly felt very tired. He yawned and lay down, continuing to suck the star.

Slowly, as he sucked, the enormous giant

began to dissolve into sand. The change began at the top of his head and moved gradually down to the tips of his great big toes.

As soon as the giant was completely turned to sand, the Magic Bee, who had been watching all along, flew down and stung the Baby.

'WAA!' screamed the Baby. He began to grow larger and larger until finally he was Nardu again. He thanked the Magic Bee again and again for her help. Remembering his promise, he picked up the Magic Pouch. He walked a few steps but then hesitated.

'Well, come on. What are you waiting for?' the Magic Pouch demanded impatiently.

'Actually', said Nardu thoughtfully, 'I don't really want to leave this place. I've spent so much of my life travelling the world trying to keep Moola happy. I think I would like to live the rest of my life here. Do you mind?' Nardu asked the Magic Pouch.

'Don't have much choice, do I?' grumbled the Magic Pouch.

'I've got a good idea', the Magic Bee chimed in. 'Nardu, you are going to be very lonely on your own. I think I could turn this pouch into a friend for you. As long as his magic doesn't clash with mine.'

The bee buzzed and then stung the Magic Pouch as gently as she could. 'Oops', she said apologetically as a large, cross-looking baby appeared. 'I'm terribly sorry, it's a baby. But don't worry, Nardu, I'm sure it will grow up in time.'

# Yael and mulwarra

Yael was a bird spirit who spent his time roaming the far reaches of the heavens. He had a long cloak of golden feathers that flowed out behind his back and up over his head to form a mask around what for humans would be eyes. However, while Yael had the body of a human he had no face. For inside the mask was nothing but endless blue sky. And although he had legs he never used them because his golden cloak was powerful enough to take him anywhere he wanted to go.

As is the case with most living things, there are both male and female bird spirits. And Yarnu, Yael's father, was desperately hoping that one day his son would settle down with one of the many female spirits who lived in the heavens. He'd tried matchmaking, but without success. As far as he knew he was the only elderly bird spirit without grandchildren.

One day, as Yael was gently hovering above Earth, he thought about how awful it must be to be human. Yael could think of nothing worse than being tied to one place by gravity. As he hovered he noticed a young girl walking along a cliff edge near the ocean. 'How strange', he said to himself. 'She's amazingly graceful for a human.' Humans were usually great, clumsy creatures who lumbered along with no respect for Mother Earth. But this girl walked carefully. She didn't thump and thud or scrape and kick. She walked slowly, too, as though she couldn't take in enough of the rugged beauty around her.

For some reason the girl must have sensed Yael's presence because she suddenly looked upwards. But at that same moment she lost her footing and plunged headlong over the cliff, down towards the sharp rocks below.

Without thinking of the consequences, Yael swooped down to catch her just in time and flew back up into the heavens with the girl in his arms.

When she opened her eyes and looked into her rescuer's empty face she gasped in fear.

'Where am I?' she moaned. 'Who are you? Am I dead?'

'No', Yael laughed. 'You're very much alive. I saved you. And in case you're wondering, I have no face because I am a bird spirit.'

'A bird spirit', she repeated. She'd heard of such things, but she'd never actually met one before.

'I suppose I should thank you', she said. 'My name is Mulwarra, and I'm a human.'

'Yes I know', he replied. 'I'm Yael.'

Yael continued to fly around with Mulwarra. He planned to return her to her home when he'd shown her what Mother Earth looked like from far above. Mulwarra was so grateful to be alive she didn't ask Yael to return her straight away.

'It's so beautiful', she sighed as she looked down at her home planet. 'So vibrant and full of life.'

'Would you like me to show you other things?' asked Yael. Spirits were used to seeing Earth from above. It was nothing new to them. But Mulwarra's enthusiasm gave him a new sense of appreciation for the things he normally took for granted.

Mulwarra nodded and soon they were soaring far, far away.

Yael and Mulwarra both lost track of time as they explored the stars, moons and planets. They found that even though he was a bird spirit and she a human they had much in common – a love of beauty and freedom.

After some time Mulwarra asked, 'Yael, why did you rescue me?'

This question made him think deeply. There was no logical reason. It had been on impulse. Yael sighed – that impulse had turned into something deeper now and he wasn't quite sure what to do about it. He decided to take Mulwarra to meet Yarnu, his father.

When Yael appeared before his father, Yarnu asked bluntly, 'What's that thing you've got in your arms?'

'I'm a human', interrupted Mulwarra bravely. She wasn't going to let this old bird spirit intimidate her.

'So you are, you poor clumsy thing', replied Yarnu pityingly. He turned to Yael and demanded, 'Why have you brought this thing of Earth here?'

Yael wanted to say, 'I'm in love!' but he wasn't sure what Mulwarra would think of that just yet, so he replied, 'She fell off a cliff and I couldn't find it in my heart to let her die'.

Yarnu looked at Yael keenly. Surely his gifted only son hadn't fallen in love with an Earthling? He decided immediately that Mulwarra must be disposed of. The thought of fat, heavy, clumsy grandchildren was too much to bear.

'Well, son, why don't you put the heavy one down and rest?' suggested Yarnu softly.

Yael refused. He knew his father well enough to know this was a trick. If he let Mulwarra go, her weight would immediately draw her back to Earth.

'You can't carry her day and night', Yarnu said crossly. 'Why don't you share the weight of her with others?'

Yael wouldn't agree to this either. His father was very powerful. One word from him and they would drop her.

'Oh, go away', Yarnu hissed angrily when he realised how determined his son was.

Yael flew off to show Mulwarra other heavenly wonders. He was very disappointed with his father. He had hoped he would understand.

Days, weeks and months passed, and Yael and Mulwarra continued their adventures, returning only now and then to see Yarnu. Yarnu waited patiently for his son to tire of the Earthling. Yarnu's wait was in vain because, against all odds, Mulwarra began to fall in love with Yael. Yarnu was filled with rage when he saw how she looked at his son. Was there no end to this nonsense, he fumed silently.

One day Mulwarra said to Yael, 'I love your world. It's very beautiful, but very different from mine'.

'But what's wrong?' asked Yael as he looked at her sad face.

'I love you, Yael', she replied, 'but I miss the feel of the earth beneath my feet. I miss the flowers

and the birds and trees. I miss my family. And . . .
I wish you had a face. I want to be able to see you
frown and be happy or sad'.

'I'd like to please you', he sighed. 'But I'm a bird
spirit, not a man.'

When Yarnu noticed that Mulwarra was unhappy and Yael depressed, he chuckled with glee.
'At last the boy is coming to his senses', he told
himself. 'It won't be long before he throws that
clumsy creature away.'

When Yael visited his father the next time
Yarnu welcomed him warmly.

'Come to your senses, have you?' he asked
eagerly, ignoring Mulwarra.

'I believe I have', replied Yael.

'Wonderful, wonderful', said Yarnu happily.
'Well, drop her off gently if you must. But when
you return I have some beautiful spirits I'd like
you to meet.'

'You don't understand, Father', said Yael. 'I
don't want to let Mulwarra go. I want to give up
my spirit form and become human. I know you
have the power to help me do it.'

Yarnu was furious. He flew around the sky in a
rage, then swooped down on Mulwarra trying
to knock her from his son's arms. Finally he
screeched, 'Leave, both of you!', and flew off into
the furthest heaven.

Yael and Mulwarra grew sadder and sadder. It
seemed there was no solution to their problem.

They no longer roamed the heavens, but sat in morbid silence holding one another.

'Hmph', complained Yarnu, who had finally returned, 'he might as well be human for all the flying he does now'.

Now Yarnu had many faults, but he loved his son deeply. He was a very strong-willed old spirit, who only wanted the best for him. It was just that his idea of best was not Yael's. He finally called Yael to him.

'If you give up this human, I'll give you anything', he offered. Yael shook his head.

'All right', the old spirit said sadly. 'I know when I'm beaten. I'll grant your request, but you know that once you leave here you can never return?'

'Yes, Father.'

'And you understand that while I can give you a human face and form, I cannot make her people accept you as you might want. Like it or not, you will never be completely one of them.'

Yael accepted this.

Yarnu spread out his own feather cloak and began to glow red – the deep, dark red of the part of Mother Earth where Mulwarra came from. The glow began to float upwards away from the old spirit and over Yael and Mulwarra. It completely enveloped them. Yael felt himself grow heavier and heavier. Before he knew it both he and Mulwarra were screaming and falling down, down, down through the heavens, past suns and planets and back to Earth. As they plunged through Earth's atmosphere the ground rushed up to meet them, but just before they hit their fall was halted and they landed gently in the sand.

When Mulwarra recovered her breath she turned to look eagerly at Yael. 'You look wonderful!' she cried. 'You're so handsome. Now I will show you the delights of my world!'

Yael smiled happily, but when he tried to walk he fell over. 'How do you move these things?' he asked as he felt his muscly legs.

'But you've always had legs', she laughed.

'I'm used to the look of them', he replied, 'but not the feel or the weight. I've never walked in my life'.

'Stand up and put one foot in front of the other', she said kindly. 'You'll soon get the hang of it.'

Yael stood up, took two paces and fell over again. They continued like that all the way along the beach. He learnt eventually, but he was never able to walk as naturally as humans. He was always a bit wobbly and he had trouble walking in a straight line.

Mulwarra's family were overjoyed to have her back. They hugged and kissed her and asked her where she'd been. When she told them they didn't really believe her. They just patted her head and decided that the poor child had been wandering around in the sun for too long.

'And who is this stranger?' they finally asked as they looked at Yael.

'This is Yael', Mulwarra replied. 'The bird spirit I was telling you about, only he's a human now and he's come to live with us.'

Her father smiled nervously at him. He didn't want to ask Yael if he really was a bird spirit just in case he said yes.

'You're welcome to stay', said Mulwarra's mother. She held out her hand, but as Yael went to take it he tripped and fell over, pulling Mulwarra's mother with him.

'He's still a bit wobbly', explained Mulwarra as she helped them both up. Her father raised his eyes to the sky. Why would a sensitive and clever girl like Mulwarra choose a man with wobbly legs? He didn't understand it at all.

Mulwarra's family tried to like Yael, but they became more and more puzzled by his strange behaviour. He wouldn't eat red meat, but loved seeds and raw worms. He'd been taken on several hunts and ruined their chances of a good catch by falling over at exactly the wrong moment. And the night they had cooked him a special meal of brush turkey he'd cried and cried. Instead of eating it, he'd gone and buried it. Indeed, it didn't matter what bird they chose to eat, Yael always wept uncontrollably when he saw the dead body.

The old men became so worried that they eventually asked Mulwarra's father to a meeting of the elders to explain why his daughter's friend was so odd.

'I have no idea', he told them sadly. 'I don't know what Mulwarra sees in him. He's always talking about the stars and deep space and . . . spirits.' He hesitated to mention the word 'spirit'. He knew it wouldn't go down well.

'What do you mean by spirits?' they asked suspiciously.

Mulwarra's father shrugged his shoulders and recounted the strange story his daughter had told him when she returned. The old men were angry that they hadn't been informed earlier. Spirits could be very bad trouble and they didn't want any of that.

'He might be an evil spirit in disguise', suggested one.

'Yes, waiting for the right moment to harm us', added another.

'But he seems harmless', said Mulwarra's father. 'It's just that he's not like the rest of us.'

'Not like the rest of us?' they repeated crossly. 'Can you think of anyone he is like?' Mulwarra's father had to agree that Yael was unlike anyone he had ever met or heard of.

'You see, that proves we're right', said the old men. 'There's no place for evil spirits here. We need to get rid of him before he causes any more trouble!'

Mulwarra's father took pity on the young lovers and warned them that it was no longer safe for them to stay. He gave them plenty of food and a good sharp spear and sent them off to find a place where they could live happily.

For days and days they followed the line of the cliff edge that ran along the ocean shore. But wherever they went people couldn't help noticing Yael's wobbly legs. And if they spoke to him they became frightened of the strange stories he told. How could a man know so much about the heavens, they reasoned, unless he was an evil spirit. And so the same old trouble would begin all over again.

One day, as they were sitting on the warm sand bathing their tired feet in the ocean, Yael said, 'I was stupid to think I could be a human. Your people will never accept me, no matter where we go'.

Mulwarra sighed. 'And yours will not accept me either', she said.

Now Yarnu, that old sticky beak of a bird spirit, had been watching his son's life grow more and more difficult. He'd been reluctantly impressed by the way Mulwarra had stuck by his son and never once criticised him. He knew he couldn't return Yael to his bird-spirit form. Even if that were possible, Yael wouldn't leave Mulwarra. However, there was one thing he could do. And he hoped it would work because it was their last chance at any real happiness.

Yarnu began to glow. This time he was blue, not red. Yael and Mulwarra sensed his presence and looked up to see a luminous, blue glow in the sky.

'It's your father', said Mulwarra.

'I wonder what he's up to', replied Yael, puzzled.

The vibrant blue glow floated out of Yarnu and down to the young couple. They were swathed in a calm, gentle light and began to feel very fluid and free and excited. The ocean waves began to cover more and more of them. They watched in surprise as their toes disappeared, then their feet, then their legs. Soon they were both part of the sea and yet still their individual selves.

'This is wonderful!' gurgled Mulwarra as she surfed through wave after wave.

'I love it!' cried Yael. 'I feel light again.' They rolled over and over frolicking and giggling like young seals.

'Thank you, Father!' they both called as he followed them out to sea.

'Be happy my two sea spirits', he said. 'I'll visit you again when my first grandchild is born.'

Then Yarnu flew off, muttering to himself, 'At least their children won't be clumsy now'. He smiled contentedly, but you couldn't see, of course, because his face went on forever. Just like the endless blue sea.

# The grumpy frog

In the beginning Australia had only one frog and he was very large and very grumpy. He hated anything getting in his way so he solved all his problems by swallowing them. This meant that each year he grew grumpier and grumpier because some of the things he ate were just not meant to be swallowed. How would your stomach feel with rocks, rainforests and mountain ranges weighing it down?

It wasn't long before the Grumpy Frog's

dreadful habit had made over half of Australia flat and featureless. There were no hills or valleys, and no giant gum trees. All that was left was hot, dry sand and one frog who was growing bigger and grumpier by the minute.

One morning, after swallowing a largish tree, he burped and grumbled, 'CROAK! I hate things getting in my way. Why can't they just move when they see me coming? I'll swallow the whole of Australia if I have to!'

'Oh dear', sighed the Good Spirit, who had been watching the Grumpy Frog with growing dismay for some time. 'What am I going to do? I can't unmake him because I never unmake anything. But he's such a problem. His head must have been upside down when I put his smile on. Perhaps that's why he's so grumpy.'

The Good Spirit watched as the Grumpy Frog continued on his way, swallowing stone after stone, tree after tree and, finally, a small hill.

'He's ruining everything', complained the Good Spirit. 'No sooner do I make something than he eats it! I wonder if he'd cheer up if I gave him a friend?'

A medium-sized, happy frog with a huge grin on his face suddenly appeared in the Grumpy Frog's pathway.

'Good morning, my dearest friend', he called cheerfully as the Grumpy Frog approached.

One gulp and he was gone. 'Urp!' burped the

Grumpy Frog. 'What a foul taste. Now I really am in a rotten mood.'

'Oh no', moaned the Good Spirit, 'now I've got a mad cannibal on my hands! Well, he's not as smart as he thinks. I'll make something so big it'll be impossible for him to swallow it'.

A towering mountain appeared right in front of the Grumpy Frog.

He croaked angrily as he swelled up with rage. 'I hate things getting in my way. Why do these things keep happening to me!' He opened his mouth wide to swallow the mountain, but his mouth was too small.

The Good Spirit smiled smugly. However, his smile soon changed to horror when he observed the Grumpy Frog burp and burp, and burp and burp again, until his mouth was one hundred times the size it had been a moment ago. It wasn't long before his mouth was so wide that he could swallow the towering mountain in one enormous gulp.

'Darn!' said the Good Spirit. 'It's that stupid stretchy skin I gave him. Why didn't I think ahead for once?'

The Good Spirit sat quietly meditating. He kept thinking, over and over, that there must be a limit to how far the Grumpy Frog could stretch.

The Good Spirit decided to keep trying. Next he placed a giant Tasmanian devil in front of the frog. GULP! It was gone. This was followed by a huge, rearing kangaroo with giant, yellow fangs, a wombat that weighed a thousand tonnes and a python long enough to stretch from the Earth to the Moon. Not one of them gave the Grumpy Frog any trouble at all.

'I'll just have to think harder', sighed the Good Spirit. 'If I don't come up with something soon he'll swallow the whole of Australia and then *I'll* be grumpy.'

Later as the Grumpy Frog continued on his not-so-merry way, he suddenly spotted a very large object ahead. He frowned and hopped closer.

'Ooooh!' he said angrily. 'It's not going to move! I just hate things getting in my way.' Stuck right in his path was the biggest, roundest fish he'd ever seen. And it was covered in tiny, pointed spikes. It was a giant blowfish, put there by the Good Spirit. In one enormous gulp the blowfish was gone. The Good Spirit waited expectantly.

Pleased that for the moment his path was clear, the Grumpy Frog hopped on. Suddenly he belched uncontrollably and his stomach began to grow.

'What's going on?' he said angrily as his stomach continued to expand. 'I'm getting bigger without eating anything!'

The blowfish was swelling up inside him. It continued to swell until the Grumpy Frog's feet began to lift off the ground. Desperately he tried to cling to the dry sand but it was just impossible.

He grew larger and larger and rose higher and higher until he was a million times his original size and was drifting into outer space. He couldn't talk or even think because his green froggy skin was stretched to its absolute limit.

The blowfish, however, had yet to reach its limit. It swelled up even more, causing its sharp spikes to poke through the Grumpy Frog's thin skin. BANG! The Grumpy Frog exploded into a million tiny pieces. Trees, rocks, mountain ranges, rainforests, animals and creatures of all shapes and sizes, including one medium-sized, happy frog, shot out into space before falling back to where they belonged in Australia.

'Aaaah', sighed the Good Spirit. 'What a relief!'

Then he closed his eyes and settled down for a nap. These kinds of problems were so exhausting.

He was just dozing off when a million tiny voices cried out, 'CROAK! We just hate things getting in our way! It makes us so cross! We'll swallow the whole of the universe if we have to!'

'What!' The Good Spirit's eyes shot open.

A million, minuscule burps echoed through space.

'Oh no!' the Good Spirit cried when he saw what had happened. 'I can't bear to look!' Dotted throughout space – on different moons, planets and asteroids – were a million tiny, grumpy green frogs who were busily swallowing everything that got in their way.

# The baby and the river spirit

The Baby yawned, opened his little eyes and looked eagerly about. It was almost morning and the first flickers of the sun's rays were just beginning to peep over the horizon.

'Goo', said the Baby as he sat up and sucked his fist.

'Goo!' he demanded more loudly.

When no one answered his call, the Baby pulled himself up, stood a moment and then wandered over to his mother. To his surprise she was still asleep, as were his grandmother and brother and everyone else.

'Ooh, goo', he said more softly.

The Baby turned and tottered on his fat legs full pelt towards the bush. He was free! There was no one awake to growl at him or tell him what to do. He could do whatever he liked.

Faster and faster the Baby staggered until he tripped over a small rock and fell flat on his face.

'WAA' he screamed angrily and pounded his little fists on the ground. 'WAA!'

'CROAK! CROAK! CROAK!' mimicked the frog, who was hiding nearby.

The Baby stopped crying and began to sniff instead. Where was that noise coming from? And who was making it?

He went back down on his hands and knees and began crawling around hunting for the noise. He lay on his stomach and peered under a small, leafy bush.

'CROAK!'

The Baby gasped in fright and pulled back.

'CROAK! CROAK!' repeated the Frog. He hopped out from under his bush shelter and looked curiously at the Baby.

'FOO!' squealed the Baby happily. He stood up and began running towards the Frog with both arms out.

Now the Frog had no idea what 'foo' meant, but he didn't like the look in the Baby's eye, so he turned and began leaping towards the river. The Baby followed, all the time calling out, 'Foo, foo!'

When they reached the river-bank the Frog quickly took one leap and disappeared under the water. The Baby waited for the Frog to come back up again, but when he didn't the Baby dived in after him.

Down, down, down the Baby plunged until he landed with a thud and a gurgle on the muddy bottom. Some fish circled him curiously. It wasn't often they found a baby sitting on the river-bed. But when his chubby little hands reached out to catch them they darted away. This made the Baby so angry that he began pounding the mud with his hands and feet.

What the Baby didn't know was that, directly underneath him, was the River Spirit, who happened to be asleep at the time.

The Baby's kicks and punches soon woke the River Spirit up.

What's going on, wondered the River Spirit as he slid out from beneath his slippery mud blanket.

Hmmn, he thought, as he peered at his attacker, a fat, strong baby.

How dare this awful little creature disturb his sleep. He'd teach him a lesson he'd never forget!

The River Spirit twisted and turned, and turned and twisted, making the waves on the surface froth and foam. Then he spun around and around, whipping the Baby back to the surface and flinging him crossly from one wave to the next. Much to the River Spirit's dismay the Baby loved every minute of it.

'Weeee', he squealed delightedly as he whizzed through the air. 'Weeeee!'

The River Spirit spun the Baby faster and faster, but it made no difference, the Baby just laughed louder and louder.

The River Spirit finally decided that instead of teaching the Baby a lesson it might be wiser to get rid of him. He knew there was a waterfall up ahead. One strong throw and his problem would be solved. However, the River Spirit gave such a mighty heave that he lost his balance and went tumbling over the waterfall too.

Down, down, down they fell with the rushing, gushing water, then on, on, on, headlong to where the river joined the ocean, and out to sea. The River Spirit hated salty water. His magic powers barely worked out of river water. He wished he'd never seen the Baby.

The River Spirit was invisible, except for the water weeds that had caught in his hair. Urged on by the thought of some new food, the Baby was quick to spy the floating bundle of weedy strands, and made a grab for them. The River Spirit cursed as the Baby took hold of the weeds – and his hair – and pulled. He twisted and turned, and turned and twisted, but the Baby would not let go. Oh no, thought the River Spirit as the Baby opened his mouth wide, he's going to eat my hair!

The Baby began to suck the strands of hair and slimy, green weed. It wasn't as delicious as milk but it was certainly better than nothing.

All the while a strong current was carrying them further and further away from land. The River Spirit looked back longingly and wondered if he would ever see his home again. Suddenly a large turtle who was also heading out to sea bumped into them. The Baby stopped sucking on the hair and weeds and inspected the Turtle eagerly. Then, still clutching the weeds and hair in one fist, the Baby reached out with his other and hoisted himself onto the turtle's neck – dragging the River Spirit with him.

The Turtle frowned. Something was clinging to her neck. She turned her head curiously and choked in astonishment at what she saw.

'A baby!' she gasped.

'Foo!' said the Baby excitedly, and tried to bite her neck.

A dangerous baby, thought the Turtle. The sooner I get rid of him the better. She quickly turned and headed for shore. She was smart enough to know that babies were land creatures.

When the River Spirit realised they had changed direction he began to hope that things would be all right after all. The Baby soon gave up trying to chomp on the Turtle's scaly neck and leant his greedy little face over the Turtle's head.

'FOO!' he said as he drooled into her lovely, bulging eyes.

The Turtle closed her eyes in horror and swam blindly for shore. She managed to beach her passengers just as the Baby was beginning to prise open one of her eyes.

The River Spirit sighed with relief as he lay on the sand. He was happy to be out of the salty water, but the sun was beginning to rise higher in the sky and he could feel his whole being starting to dry out.

'Foo', said the Baby quietly, and he began stuffing the River Spirit's weed-entwined hair back into his mouth.

The River Spirit closed his eyes in despair. He was shrinking from dehydration and soon he would be bald as well. What else could possibly happen?

Just then a kangaroo came hopping out from the bush. When the Kangaroo saw the seaweed-eating Baby she jumped over and inspected him curiously.

How strange to find a baby here all alone, she thought.

She bent down to sniff him, and as she did so the Baby looked up and grabbed hold of her tender nose with his free hand. The kangaroo reared back, pulling the Baby, and the River Spirit, with her. Frantically she shook her head from side to side but the Baby would not let go. Up and down she jumped on the spot until the Baby's grip was loosened and he flew into the air. Instead of landing back on the sand, both he and the River Spirit fell head first into her pouch!

This made the Kangaroo so angry that she headed back into the bush at a cracking pace. The Baby began to giggle loudly because her fur was tickling his skin, while the River Spirit wriggled wildly because he felt so cramped.

After hopping for a long time the Kangaroo stopped beside a river to catch her breath and have a drink of water. As she bent down to drink, the River Spirit peeped out of her pouch and recognised his very own river. It's now or never, he thought to himself. He peered back at the Baby. The Baby had finally been rocked to sleep by the ride and was no longer clasping the River Spirit's hair. The River Spirit dived out of the pouch and slid into the water. He floated down gently to the soft, murky bottom, where he slipped beneath his mud blanket, vowing never to go near another baby as long as he lived.

When the Kangaroo finished drinking, she looked down at the sleeping child in her pouch. She felt a little sorry for him. He was only a baby after all. Then she remembered a clearing close by where people sometimes camped. I'll drop him off there, she decided. Someone will find him eventually.

The Kangaroo jumped slowly into the clearing, which happened to be the very one where the Baby's family was camped. She stopped and leant forward as far as she could. The Baby rolled over twice in her pouch, then gently slipped out onto the ground.

'Foooo', he said drowsily as he lay on the grass. He stuck his fist in his mouth and was soon fast asleep again.

In a little while the Baby's family woke up. His mother was surprised to see her baby son still sleeping.

'It's not like him to sleep this late', she said to his grandmother. 'He's normally the first one up and into mischief.'

'Oh, how can you talk about him like that?' protested his grandmother. 'Let him sleep a bit longer. He's such a sweet, innocent little thing!'

# Glossary

**bardi grub**    edible, wood-boring grub

**barramundi**    large, fresh-water fish

**bat-hole**    wombat-hole

**billabong**    an inland water-hole

**blowfish (or toadfish)**   self-inflating, poisonous fish

**bungarra**    a lizard

**dillybag**    bag made of twisted grass used for carrying food or personal belongings

**echidna**    a small spine-covered animal with a long, slender snout

**goanna**    a large lizard

**gumnut**    seed capsule from a eucalypt (gum) tree

| | |
|---|---|
| **kangaroo paw** | plant with a flower like the paw of a kangaroo |
| **numbat** | small reddish brown animal with a long bushy tail and white stripes |
| **spinifex** | spiny-leaved, tussock-forming grass |
| **Sturt's desert pea** | Australian plant with brilliant scarlet and black flowers |
| **Tasmanian devil** | ferocious, carnivorous marsupial |
| **witchetty grub** | fat, white, edible grub |
| **wokkaburra** | heavy, shaped wooden object sometimes used for fighting |
| **yam** | vegetable, similar to a potato, with a pink flesh |
| **yamilli creeper** | poisonous plant |

# About the author

Sally Morgan was born in Perth, Western Australia, in 1951. She is a full-time painter and writer.

For as long as she can remember Sally wanted to paint and write. However, at school she was discouraged from expressing herself through her art because her teachers failed to see the promise in her individual style. It was not until she researched her family history and discovered her Aboriginal identity that she found meaning in her images, and gained the confidence to pick up her paints again.

Sally's first book, *My Place*, which tells of the discovery of her Aboriginal ancestry, is now an international bestseller and won the first Order of Australia Association Book Prize in 1989. In the same year, Sally's second book, *Wanamurraganya*, received the Human Rights and Equal Opportunities Commission Award for Literature. Sally's paintings and screen prints have won many awards and her art is represented in galleries and private collections in Australia and the United States.